LADY HARROW

This is a work of fiction. Any slights of people, places, or organizations are unintentional.

First printing 2019

ISBN 978-1-7323457-1-3

LADY HARROW

Robert Duke

The adventure that started it all!
Book One in the Mortal Orders Series is available now

SHATTERBUG

As an enigmatic foe lurks in the shadows, follow Marco Nieve in his quest to uncover the secrets of the titular time-travelling suit, in order to prevent a tragic future he has only begun to glimpse, and in doing so, become the first hero his world will know.

Visit www.mortalorders.com to order your copy today!

Contents

Issue 1
These Things Do Happen

"Time?" Heraldo asked of the younger man standing beside him.

The man twisted his arm into his pocket so as to avoid touching the gun resting in his waistband. He pulled his phone out just enough to turn the screen on, cocking it slightly to glance down at it.

"10:37." he replied to the lieutenant.

"We'll give them to 10:45, and then we're outta here." Heraldo lamented. His distributor had been the one to arrange this meeting, so one would think they would be the one who was early. Yet here he was; a Del Toro lieutenant and his crew of enforcers, waiting around on a Tuesday night when they could be hitting the Strip.

But despite his declaration, Heraldo Rendón wasn't looking to leave in a hurry. He had a vested interest in seeing this distributor tonight, and was thankful the higher-ups in his 'organization' had selected him to see what the Menteur wanted. Heraldo had long been convinced that the eccentric drug trafficker had been skimming product not only from the Del Toros, but from most of the other street gangs in Las Vegas, selling what he stole from one group to all the others, all the while stealing from them.

1

He wasn't sure how, but after taking a look at their last supply, there was no doubt in his mind.

Finally, a faint knocking sounded on the door leading into the back room they sat in. This auto shop wasn't a major outpost for the Del Toros, being well outside their territory, but they had the connections to make use of it now and then for private affairs like this.

Rendón nodded to one of the other enforcers on his crew to go check it out, as he sat in his torn-up swivel chair, facing the door. Were he not covered by his boys, or armed himself, he'd be exceptionally vulnerable. But that was how he liked it. Heraldo had gotten where he was by playing it fast and loose, and getting results anyway.

The thug returned with an unusually excited man in a silvery three-piece suit and a woman in attire slightly more appropriate for the environment. Naturally, Heraldo paid just a bit more attention to the latter.

She wore a leather jacket, unzipped and open, over a red shirt that ended above her stomach. It was the middle of summer; it made sense to uncover some parts, especially if one insisted on wearing such a heavy coat. Looked like real leather, too. Her black pants hugged her tightly, making it quite clear that she was very athletic. He'd hate to be caught alone with her. Or, maybe he wouldn't. Her brown hair was dyed slightly red, and she had a firm, no-nonsense face. It was a darker complexion, her skin not too far from his own in shade. However, her eyes gave away more of a Native American background than a Hispanic one.

Still, Heraldo returned his attention to the man, the Menteur, who he was more eager to confront. Women were too much trouble anyway, and killing her boss wouldn't make for a very good first impression.

"Sorry for the delay," the Menteur began. His French accent was awful; Heraldo knew he was just some scrawny American. But in this line of business, one had to make concessions to get results, and so everyone tended to humor the wealthy supplier. "We had passed by here twice trying to find you; it just seemed so... vulgar. We couldn't believe it was the right place."

"Cute." Rendón replied shortly. "Now, why did you need to see us?"

"Hold on now, this is a little unfair, isn't it?" the peculiar man said, motioning to the five Del Toro men flanking Heraldo.

"You were the one who said 'enforcers only'. Not our fault you only have the one. She looks pretty capable anyway, so I don't know why you're complaining."

"No, no, this simply isn't acceptable. We'll have to schedule this arrangement for another time." The Menteur clicked his fingers and turned to leave, indicating to the woman to follow. She turned coyly, and they started to march out.

"Hey! No games, *Frenchy.*" Heraldo stood up with this, and his enforcers all placed a hand on their holstered pieces. "I didn't say you could go."

"We have nothing to discuss if you insist on being so... *injuste.*" he replied, turning his head back only slightly as he continued his exit.

"Circle him." the lieutenant ordered his men. They did as instructed, trapping the Menteur and his lady enforcer in the back room. "Actually, we have a lot to discuss."

"No, I don't think—"

"Look at me!" Heraldo shouted.

3

Startled, the Menteur turned to the Del Toro officer. "Oh?"

"Yeah. Cause I know your deal, Menteur. I know you've been selling product skimmed from our supplies to the Russians and the Chinese, and that you've been shorting them to sell back to us. I've confirmed with everyone; your drugs show up, get counted, everything's cool, then a bunch vanishes, and suddenly you've got the same amount going to someone else."

The overdressed man maintained his composure at the accusation, but proceeded to ask, "And what led you to this conclusion, then?"

"The funniest thing, actually." Heraldo pulled out his phone. "Internet's a wonderful thing, you find the strangest information by total accident. I got curious what the Menteur meant. I always assumed it was mentor or teacher or whatever, and found—if you can believe it—that it's nothing like that at all. You know what Menteur is French for?"

The Menteur smiled. "Enlighten me."

Heraldo—and his heart—skipped a beat.

"Liar."

The Del Toro enforcers all pulled out their pistols and aimed them for the Menteur. Quickly and simultaneously, they all began firing on the lying drug trafficker.

At the same time, the woman revealed she had been packing as well; a comedically large-barreled pistol appeared in her hands, and as she squeezed the trigger over and over again, turning with each shot, she landed on Heraldo's men with pinpoint accuracy, the force of the larger bullets throwing them off balance and knocking them to the ground, bleeding. Knock after knock of hammers hitting gunpowder and shriek after shriek of bullets streaking through the air echoed in the concrete room. Watching the Menteur's enforcer work was a terrifying experience, like some violent performance just for Heraldo.

When the room was silent again, all of Rendón's enforcers were on the ground. He and the woman were standing, guns trained on each other. The Menteur was still and unharmed. No one had hit him.

Heraldo was shocked. Without realizing it, his gun was shaking in his hands. Noting this, the Menteur's enforcer lowered her weapon and walked over to him cautiously, but with an air of triumph. He could still see the smoke rising out of the holes in his men.

When she reached him, she flicked his gun to the ground with her hand, and held hers up again—pressed against his forehead.

"What— what are you, lady?"

She smiled, then frowned. "My *name* is Lady Harrow."

She pulled her trigger.

The weapon clicked. It was empty.

"Now run along, little boy. And tell your superiors that the Menteur expects a little more compliance from the Del Toros moving forward. He's got big plans for expansion that'll benefit all of us, if you stay alive."

He did as instructed, stumbling over his fallen enforcers and out the door into the auto shop, then back to his car parked outside.

"Excellent work, my dear." The Menteur congratulated his enforcer.

"Oh, shut up." Lady Harrow replied, unenthused. She threw her gun across the room.

Before it hit the wall, it dissolved into a cloud of dust, dispersing back into the air.

She looked to her employer, who stood there blinking with confusion, before he too began to fade away. Pieces of his suit fell off as he changed state, returning to dust and air. His face sifted back into his head, and as his legs vanished, the whole of the Menteur collapsed, becoming a cloud of scattered particles; then those, too, became nothing.

She looked around at the Del Toro gang members on the ground. The smoke rising from their bullet holes now became dust rising from the pools of their blood, which disappeared like the illusions they always had been. As Harrow looked from above at the one nearest her, the wound from her imaginary gun became little more than a ruffle in his shirt. None of them were harmed; their minds believed they'd been fatally shot, so their bodies reacted accordingly. The human brain was so easy to convince.

Finally, Lady Harrow held her own hand up to her eyes, and watched as her fingers dissolved away, taking the red nail polish and fancy rings along with them. She lost sight of it as her eyes folded back into her head, becoming dust as well. Her chest crumbled into chunks of insignificant debris, and the rest of her body followed suit until even that illusion was just a memory.

The real Lady Harrow entered now, her illusions having fully dissipated. The trial had proceeded exactly as planned.

She walked over to Heraldo's weapon on the floor; a custom-engraved pistol signifying a mediocre rank in the Del Toros. Not mediocre to them, of course. She tucked it into the back of her already tight pants, then walked back out of the auto shop and into the open air of Avilla Park in Las Vegas, Nevada.

Harrow fished in her jacket pocket for the keys to the black sedan parked along the right side of the building, pressing the button to unlock it. 'The Menteur' didn't need to be anywhere else tonight, so she was more than ready to head home.

The drive back home was simpler than her false employer's description of their arrival made it seem. The auto shop was right on a wide main road, and one turn from there onto another similar street let her follow that most of the way. From there, it was easy to navigate back to the Arts District, especially late at night when there was minimal traffic. Only the Strip remained awake and booming at all hours; the actual city of Las Vegas was like any other.

An uneventful drive to an unremarkable parking lot was enough to have Lady Harrow's eyes falling just slightly. She stepped out of and locked her car before beginning her short walk around the back of the building.

She could see that the small cocktail bar at the end of the outlet was still open, though not very busy. They advertised live music, but weren't booked every night. She silently thanked no one in particular that she would be able to fall straight to sleep without incessant drumming and singing.

As she passed by the alley between her building and the Thai restaurant that shared the parking lot—which had been treated to a bit of landscaping in some trees and decorative rocks—some rustling caught her eye in the dark.

7

Harrow strained her eyes to try and get an idea of what was moving. The light from the street lamps overhead was angled just enough to be useless in this situation only, and the gallery on this end of her building was long empty; no exterior lights remained on to help her.

At last, her persistence was rewarded. Whatever was hiding in the shadows turned to look back at her. She recoiled in surprise as the figure's face came into view.

It was a twisted and empty face. Greyed and dead. Its cheeks were beginning to decay, and much of its hair had fallen out; along with the skin that held it to its skull, which was now exposed under a layer of brown, dried blood. Its eyes were empty, though Lady Harrow couldn't tell if the eyeballs had simply fallen out or were clouded with shade and despair. It snarled pitifully before retreating into the darkness. The sounds of its shambling footfalls told Harrow it was escaping down the alley.

Her body's instinct took hold, and she found herself chasing the horror out of the garden-like space and out across the poorly-lit and abandoned street.

Despite this, her mind was struggling with what she had just witnessed. Surely this couldn't be her nightmares again? She hadn't experienced visions like this in years. She idly patted her back pocket, ensuring her lucky charm was still there. It was— thank goodness. And yet that reassurance was temporary, it didn't answer the question as to how this was here. Could the charm be failing? Or was this thing—which all evidence and prior experience could only conclude should be a hallucination—real after all? Lady Harrow didn't know whether to trust her mind at that moment. All she knew was that she had to chase the thing.

The creature ahead of her made a slight to the left. Although it was dragging its feet, and was hampered by torn clothes and, of course, rotting flesh, it was fast. Harrow was keeping pace well, but only just. She did have the advantage of seeing where it was going, and was able to make more immediate and precise turns than the fleeing horror.

It ducked into another alley beside a small museum. It moved hastily past the cars parked in the tiny dirt lot there, then bolted out the other end, onto a much larger road: Main Street of the Arts District.

Lady Harrow stopped at the sidewalk's edge. The ghoul was halfway across the road, but two cars were approaching from the right. The headlights of another prodded at Harrow's peripheral vision on the left. She wouldn't be able to even meet the creature halfway. Although this road was better lit than the one they had just crossed, she was wearing all black, and there was no intersection nearby to provide extra illumination. She watched the shambling mess quickly hobble further across, as the two oncoming cars crept ever closer.

She knew it would be wishful thinking to hope they would hit the monster, and she was right. It was already safely across by the time they whisked by. The car to her left flew past her, too, and she took the opportunity to make up for lost time.

Her feet fell hard on the asphalt as she broke into as much of a sprint as she could muster.

But, she felt a familiar light intrude upon her vision to the left, and turned her head just in time to see a car heading straight for her. She stopped hard.

The driver must have slammed their brakes as they turned harshly to the left, trying to dodge the unseen pedestrian. Harrow had failed to take into account the bend in the road on her left, and so didn't see the second car approaching. She threw her face back in the direction of the creature, but it was nowhere in sight. The distraction had cost her the chase.

The car that nearly hit her had continued after recovering, and so she was left alone in the middle of the road. She jogged briskly back to the sidewalk, and began a defeated walk back home, making every attempt to hold herself together until she knew she was safe. She couldn't think now, couldn't escape into her mind here.

Now on the correct side of her building, Harrow approached a brick wall. The graffiti here was extensive. Uncharacteristic of the area, though she felt it wasn't out of place in terms of quality; it was the Arts District, after all. It was a symbol of a planet and three moons, with a ring depicted as cutting away at part of the planet. It was clean and sharp, a perfect circle, and by manufacturing the appearance of a ring with a lack of paint, rather than small triangles at the edges of the planet, or just a different color, it created a pleasingly minimalist display. She was very proud of it, although it didn't take much in the way of talent. It appeared exactly as she imagined it.

She flicked her hand aside—although casually, not out of necessity—to bid the illusion to dissolve.

The wall obeyed. The paint began to crack and fade, fluttering off of the bricks as though time were washing it away before her eyes. The mortar between the bricks started to sag, before sifting into the spaces of its own vanishing, falling back to the ground before dissipating. The bricks, unsupported, began to topple on and over each other, with more of the material breaking away with each resounding *clink* of clay impacting clay. The wall fell away into dust, and then into nothing. The hole it left behind granted Lady Harrow passage into her small studio of a home.

As she passed through the threshold, she once again turned her hand for effect as she rebuilt the wall in her mind. Her power followed her mental assembly, and all at once the wall was reformed where it had been just moments ago, complete with the graffiti planet on the other side. An illusion to keep out unwanted intruders to her modest living space.

Harrow sat down on her bed in the center of the room. She began to fish inside her mind, weaving together images and scents and noises to create a sense of harmony among the synapses of her brain. She was very familiar with this concept, now, but it required absolute focus. Once every infinite piece of her consciousness was at her disposal, and working in tandem, she was able to lay down new instructions, new rules for her mind to follow as second nature. Specifically, she willed herself to maintain the illusion of her graffiti wall without actively thinking about it. It would remain visible and sturdy until she dismissed it.

She looked around her modest living space. It wasn't rugged by any means; she had procured numerous extravagant trophies in furnishings and decorations over her time as a seasoned criminal. But, it was eclectic and sparse. The bed, a large wardrobe and vanity, a full-length mirror, and an executive desk were the only large pieces of furniture. There wasn't even a table, or any chairs. There was never any need for such things; she never had guests, and always ate at nice restaurants. She had plenty of spending money, after all, living rent-free on ill-gotten gains.

The memory of that creature—that zombie—was still fresh in her mind, though. She couldn't trust that it was real on faith alone. Yet, she wasn't even sure whether she wanted it to be real, or her nightmares seeping through again, like they had in her youth.

She once again gathered all of the portions of her brain to work in unison. She idly pulled her lucky charm from her back pocket and held it in her hand. Even without looking at it, she could recall it in haunting detail.

It wasn't anything particularly special in terms of craftsmanship. She'd stolen it from a tourist trap of a gift shop when she first ran away, simply because it looked pretty and she could. It was a simple keychain—or had been; the chain and key ring had fallen off ages ago—of a globe, circumscribed in a sterling silver ring so as to spin. The model of Earth inside had a plastic casing which had clouded with considerable wear over the years. But she could still recognize the imperfect shapes of the continents. Each landmass was a fragment of a different mineral, and so they only approximated their actual visage against the blue agate representing the oceans. Granted, even maps were approximations of their actual visage, to a certain degree. It was a cheap souvenir. But it had come to mean everything to her. The one possession she couldn't bear to lose.

More important in the moment, it was the object upon which she tethered her most vital of mental instructions. It served as a phylactery of sorts, a thing to make the binds placed upon her mind physical. It was around this simple globe that she tied all of her thoughts and emotions, to keep herself from subconsciously using her powers to create nightmares to terrorize her, as they had done for more than half of her life; until she learned this trick. Most permanent routines placed in her mind didn't require a conduit; her wall was one such example. But imaginary subroutines so powerful and important, that so seriously affected the foundations of her consciousness and her way of life, were too much of a burden to carry without aid.

And so, Harrow fished around inside her mind once more, seeking out the tethers placed upon her thoughts and wrapped around the globe in her fingers.

They were unwavering.

Her nightmares were still under control.

Again, though, she was unsure whether to be relieved or not. She hoped she would be able to sleep soundly enough so as to make that decision in the morning.

Lady Harrow changed into her pajamas, washed her face in the tiny bathroom—which itself was not a separate room, but rather a private area of the studio-like space that she called home—and returned to her bed. She willed an illusion of a small brick to fall onto the light switch, and even though she could no longer see, she felt the brick dissolve and disappear into the darkness. Satisfied, she allowed herself to relax and drift to sleep.

Issue 2
The Ghost

Lady Harrow wasted no time getting down to business the next day. Rather than rack her brain on the possibility of some kind of zombie outbreak in the heart of Las Vegas, she opted to take the initiative and investigate the situation.

Of course, she wasn't a detective. She had to keep up appearances among the criminal class she associated herself with. It was important to keep the Menteur relevant, a fiction though he was. But, she thought, perhaps she could use her standing in the city underbelly to her advantage in this endeavor.

She began with her usual Wednesday routine. As Fridays were optimal shipping days for her operation's illicit products, she would spend the days leading up to the weekend going to each of the main dealers from the local gangs to gauge their needs. Today would begin with the Del Toro dealers—this was why she had arranged her meeting with Heraldo the night before. Now—with their new 'understanding'—she would be in a better position not only in maintaining her cover as the Menteur's representative, but also in the movement of her product.

Granted, none of Lady Harrow's product was real. As the Del Toro lieutenant had noted, some portion of most of her shipments were sophisticated illusions, cleverly made permanent with mental ties to the physical parts of the order, which shattered when they were unsealed. Those parts themselves were made up of a tiny fraction of basic grounds of low-effect pharmaceuticals, doctored with an assortment of cheap cooking ingredients for texture—totally harmless whether snorted, ingested, or injected, but convincing nonetheless. She simply ensured that the product checked and tested by the gang receivers was of the imaginary variety, and let the faults of the human mind do the rest.

This dealer operated out of a rather large Laundromat. There were always a number of young men and women loitering outside, so there was no question in the eyes of the criminally initiated of what this place was actually being used for. Of course, the transactions inside were handled with care and secrecy.

She approached the Del Toros hanging about outside their station.

Harrow nodded to one of the younger men—a boy nicknamed Kicks for his unusually detailed knowledge of the history of popular footwear. "Hey, Kicks."

"*M'lady.*" he said half-ironically, bowing slightly to maintain his position on the wall he leaned against. Most of the people she knew by name referred to her in this way. Being teased was part of having a nickname in this kind of culture.

"Lemme talk to you about something when I finish up in here." she said with a friendly, if concerned smile.

"Uh, sure. *Lo tienes*, I'll be here." he replied. Naturally he was somewhat confused. Harrow rarely had conversations that weren't business related.

She continued inside, turning to the counter as she did to meet her contact's eyes. The attendant noticed and returned to her work. No signals, just a silent understanding between two professionals. Harrow walked down the aisle of washing machines to the seating area at the back of the establishment.

The Del Toro gang controlled a small but important part of the Vegas drug trafficking industry. Lady Harrow considered them her most important clients, even though they were not her largest source of income. Their range extended from the eastern end of the downtown area out along the south side of the 515 until it turned south. On that axis, they dealt in the areas down to East Sahara Drive. They weren't right on the Strip or even directly adjacent, but they were close enough to get business from the gambling patronage, without being inclined to raise their prices to keep demand within their supply. A proverbial sweet-spot both geographically and economically.

Because of this, they served as an ideal target of Harrow's long game. She now had enough pull among the other local small-time dealers and gangs in the area, and the resources of both physical and intangible varieties, to start working more closely with the Del Toros. Specifically, she wanted to pump them up, make them a bigger name with a bigger territory and bigger profits, slowly becoming their only supplier while leaning away from her other clients, and in fact, helping them to choke out their competition and claim their territory, eventually leading to the Strip. With her business so fully integrated into the monopolistic empire of the Del Toros, the demand for hard drugs would remain, but it would be met with a completely false supply. The city would be cured of its epidemic without even realizing it.

For now, though, the Menteur's business was still one of many suppliers in a diverse drug trafficking trade. She was ready to move forward in her plan now, but her ultimate goals were still quite a ways away.

Lady Harrow was pulled from her wishful thinking of the future by the company of her contact.

Jenna was the manager of the Laundromat, and a dealer for the Del Toros. Heraldo was technically her superior, but she was largely left to her own devices when it came to her business in the area. The exception to that was with regards to what she was allowed to pay for product. That was dictated by the lieutenants. And now, Harrow expected, she would be more willing to write a bigger check to the Menteur, especially after hearing out his enforcer.

"Heard you had a good time with Rendón last night, H." she said with a casual smile. Jenna was almost all business—much like Harrow herself—but the two had a bantering relationship now after having worked together for so long.

"Oh, he told you about that?" She was interested to hear his version of events, and see whether more action needed to be taken against his reservations.

"Just that you were pretty convincing, and a real animal."

Harrow smiled. She figured he would probably imply they had slept together. Even in the losing position, it was still important for men's egos to have such a card for power plays. Of course, she didn't mind with Jenna. She knew all too well the psychology of men and their stories.

"Oh yeah. He's not too good of a shot though, if I'm honest."

The two chuckled briefly before their faces returned to those of serious demeanor.

"So what are you looking at this week, J? Two cases again?" Harrow suggested.

"Honestly might have to do just half a case this weekend. We've barely touched your last supply. Not a big laundry group this past week or two."

"Wow, sounds like it. Alright, I can handle that. Now, the boss's figures did go up a bit, I don't know if Heraldo—"

"He mentioned that that came up, yeah." Jenna interrupted expectantly. She wasn't upset, just prepared. "I figured fifteen percent? Already got it counted up."

"Actually, just seven." she lied. Harrow liked Jenna, and although she was planning for more of a twelve percent increase, she figured she could afford to cut her a deal. "He's got some big expansion plan going so he's asking for a smidge more from everyone to be fair."

"That'll work. I'll be right back, in that case." she replied, standing up from the small table and walking to the back offices.

Harrow lost herself in idle thought while she waited on the admittedly attractive woman. She always wondered what a relationship would be like for her. Unfortunately, there was never any way it would work, despite her feelings. It just wasn't the right environment for someone like her, and she knew that.

Jenna returned after a few short minutes with a grocery bag full of boxes. They were of course filled with cash, and the two had a strong enough work relationship that Harrow trusted everything was in order, and so made no effort to check it here.

As Harrow walked out, she turned to see her contact's smile. "Bye, H!"

"See ya, J!" she replied, before stepping through the sliding door and back into the heat of the Sonora Desert.

18

She turned to her right to see that Kicks was still leaning against the wall. "You got a minute?"

"Yeah, yeah." he said as she stepped closer. They were cleverly under the shade of the building, so Harrow felt no need to put her sunglasses on, even though it was shining brightly on the lot in the corner of her eye. "What's up, *chica*?"

She smiled through firm eyes, as if to say 'really?', but continued anyway. "I wanted to ask: have you seen any sort of strange things lately? Like at night?"

Kicks' eyes squinted more than they already were. "I don't get it. Strange how? It's Vegas, baby!" He tried to sound aloof and joking, but he seemed genuinely confused upon reading Harrow's face.

"I mean like, weird animals, or, say..." She hesitated. "Monsters."

He squinted again, before his eyes widened. He hunched over slightly, as if to hide from the sun even further, and replied with a hushed tone. "Did you see it, too?"

"I don't know," she said, matching his position and voice. "What did you see?"

"I didn't see much, man." he said with audible concern. "It was late and dark; I was just watching TV in *mis abuelas* house. I turned to look outside even though I couldn't see anything, and there was this... like a dude just hobbling on the road. But fast, man. And then it turned, and I didn't see no eyes at all. Like some *monstruo*."

Lady Harrow's breathing had stopped and her heart sank with anxiety. The description was spot on. Even through his poorly

19

worded description, the image pierced her thoughts as she saw her own encounter all over again. "And then what?"

"And then it ran off. I figured I was already drunk off my ass, I threw my can away and fell asleep right there. But I heard stories from some of the others. It's scary."

"What did they see?" She had to make an effort to not sound angry, but she was demanding to know more. She needed to know.

"I mean it's all rumors, I don't know how much of it's true. But one of the guys over at the community center says he tried to chase one down and two more cut him off. They held him and looked him dead in the eyes like a warning, and then ran off like crazy people. And he said their eyes were like *el abismo*.

"And then this *chica* I know from *mis abuelas* neighborhood—it's not important how I know her, but I do—she swears one was right up on her doorstep one night. She was about to shoot it, but it swiped at her and ran off. She said it was like one of those zombies from that movie where they were fast. But it didn't look gross, just... Well, she said *pésimo*. Appalling. And it scared her like nothing else did before."

So what Harrow saw *was* real. And it was worse than she thought: there were many of them. They were few and far between, but with that much distance between sightings, and that much boldness to come out where people can see them multiple times... this was a serious concern. She needed to know more.

"Thank you, Kicks." She hugged him, though even she wasn't sure why. He hugged back, shaking slightly. Or maybe that was her. "It'll be ok. I'm going to look into it."

20

She let go, and started to walk away. She turned back to Kicks before she got to her car. "Tell your lady friend she won't have to worry about it anymore!"

It was the same story with the crew at the smaller operation at the southern end of the Del Toro territory. Running out of a tiny third-party phone retailer, the dealer there was regretful in only needing to buy half his usual order, citing a decline in interest over the past few weeks. And then, the other employees there involved in the local ring had their own stories of dark creatures and shambling not-quite people. If they hadn't personally seen one, they claimed to know someone who had.

And again, from the small-time dealers that the Del Toros allowed to sell in their territory. They weren't able to purchase nearly as much product as usual, and they each had a sighting to share from the darker parts of the city.

From all of these rumors and stories and hearsay, Lady Harrow was able to put together a somewhat clearer picture of what she had seen.

These creatures—which always resembled tattered and beaten people, devoid of life and light—moved quickly and without thought, like animals. They generally seemed to skulk, and in these cases usually appeared alone. In groups, they behaved more like scavengers, hanging around warehouses or collections of garbage and junk. They didn't seem to take much though; they searched, but rarely found anything, as far as their observers could tell.

They were also fiercely protective, but uninterested in harming anyone, only scaring them enough so as to escape back into the shadows. They looked like zombies, but their behavior was simultaneously erratic and calculated; noticeably nonviolent, in a feral sort of way.

21

Armed with what she believed was about as much information as she was going to be able to get, and having finished with her runs for the Del Toros for the morning, Harrow retired to her car to head to lunch. She hoped she would be able to make a plan to tackle this situation over a nice French cuisine.

As the black sedan sped off, another woman eyed it carefully from nearby. She pulled her sunglasses down her nose just slightly so as to better see the license plate on the stranger's car. She had overheard the Native American woman talking to one of the lowlifes in the area, who she knew to be a drug dealer, and was quite intrigued by the stories they'd exchanged.

She began to walk in the same direction, musing to herself in her head. An undead outbreak in the underbelly of Las Vegas, and a self-righteous young woman brave enough to question it. This was a situation she could find herself getting deeply involved in.

Issue 3
Spellbound

The Grand Canal Shoppes was hardly the most upscale location in Las Vegas, although it tried very hard to pretend to be. It was by no means a slum, to be sure, but an experienced and intelligent person could see past its illusions and recognize it for what it truly was: a well painted American Mall.

Still, Lady Harrow did enjoy coming here. She couldn't deny the atmosphere, and the food—though more simple than it appeared or was priced for—was plenty satisfying. She was especially fond of the French restaurant here; it was her favor for their *Mussels Marinière* that inspired her in the characterization of her ersatz employer. This was the meal she chose to enjoy for lunch today, having finished her rounds with the Del Toro contacts.

She thought more about the information she had collected, and her next steps. Logically, finding another of the mysterious horrors and successfully following it as it fled would be the ideal. However, that was easier said than done. Although her reports seemed to indicate they often appeared in the presence of criminals and scum, whom most of society politely ignored, it was still an irregular pattern.

Harrow created a tiny illusion on her napkin—an approximation of the southern parts of Las Vegas—upon which she could map those claimed incidents.

First, of course, was her encounter in the Arts District. She let a small dot glow on that portion of her model.

Kicks' grandmother lived in the Del Toro territory, not far from Jenna's Laundromat. His lady friend also lived in that community, though exactly where she was unsure of. She willed that whole block to glow for her, to be safe.

The community center was between the two, closer to the freeway. She placed a dot there, although it was unclear from Kicks' story whether it was seen there, or just by someone who worked there.

She recalled all of the stories she'd been told, figuring out where all these creatures had been seen and marking them. When she was done, she was left with a disturbing picture.

It was nothing. Chaos. Pointlessness. There was no rhyme or reason; they were just there, all around, hiding in the dark spaces. Looking for something, apparently—but none of the locations had anything in common.

As she tugged at her hair with one hand and fiddled with her lucky globe on the table with the other—head hung over the napkin her map was projected on—someone pulled out the seat across the two-person table on the 'outside' patio of the French restaurant. She instinctively let the illusion fall, and blew a quiet breath downward to kick-start brushing away the dust left behind, giving it time to vanish before being noticed.

"Do I know you?" Lady Harrow asked with some intentional attitude as her head bolted up. She leaned back in her chair to get a good look at the figure sitting down opposite her.

The woman was tall and lean, much like her. She was quite dark skinned, and her facial structure was more reminiscent of

African ancestry than Native American or Hispanic. She had long dark hair, straightened and shining under the lights in the painted ceiling. Her clothes were less intense than Harrow's, coming off more preppy than hardened—she was clearly a materialistic woman—and yet she had the audacity to sit with a stranger in a leather jacket without a word.

"I'm Legacy. Now you know me." she replied. Although it was a snarky comeback, there was no attitude in her voice. She sounded genuinely interested in making a connection. "What can I call you?"

"Lady Harrow." She maintained her position, audibly inviting the stranger to leave. Still, she remained, her arms resting on the table.

"I saw you talking to those boys. About the things."

At this, Harrow perked up slightly, though didn't give it away. "What's it to you?"

Legacy reached one hand hesitantly towards Harrow's, grazing it. A solemn kind of fear invaded the very edges of her eyes, and from the way she tried to avert her gaze, Harrow believed it to be unintentional and legitimate. "I've seen one. A few, actually."

Harrow was excited now. She had just stumbled on potentially more information. Better, it had come looking for her. She hoped this would bring more clues as to where to begin her hunt.

Before she could ask a question, though, the woman grabbed hold of her hand more assuredly. "Are you trying to get rid of them?"

"I'm... going to try to, certainly." She was taken aback by the stranger's sudden questioning of her own. Although she remained skeptical, Harrow let herself relax some. "First I need to find them. Where did you see them? What were they doing?"

The waiter came to drop off Harrow's bill. She pretended to fish into her jacket pocket idly, but was actually conjuring an illusion of cash to set down with the check. Through this, she held eye contact with Legacy.

"Just around. Late at night, sorta skulking. I never got close to them, I just watched. They were sniffing and picking things up and putting them down, or sometimes carrying them away—but it was dark so I couldn't quite see what. Sometimes big things, usually little."

The waiter came back to pick up the check with Harrow's cash. As he walked away, Harrow held her gaze with the expositing woman. Legacy, however, allowed her eyes to shift just a bit to the leaving service staff. She glanced just in time to see the money start to fade into dust.

Lady Harrow saw her eyes widen, but wasn't sure why. She turned her head for a glimpse of what Legacy had seen, but the woman's words were an unexpected jolt.

"Oh, shit." Legacy whispered. "You're a Telignen!"

Harrow's head quickly swiveled back to her dining partner. Her hands rushed to her lap, her heart skipped a beat, and her mouth fell agape. The look on her face was of confusion and fear, more than shock. "How do you know that word?"

Legacy stood up and held her hand out to Lady Harrow. "Come with me; we definitely have a lot to talk about."

She was still uneasy. All Harrow had wanted was to eat her mussels in peace. Instead, she found someone willing to provide more information on the dark creatures, and was inexplicably discovered in a place and by a person that shouldn't even be able to comprehend her, much less identify her.

Her skepticism and hesitation washed away quickly, though. If this Legacy knew what a Telignen was, she may be in a unique position to help her discover the truth of the zombies, and be of use in getting rid of them. Perhaps this woman knew more than she initially let on, but would now feel more open to sharing.

Lady Harrow took Legacy's hand, and the two stepped out of the gated indoor patio and walked along the canal, toward the elevators to the Palazzo.

Issue 4
Into the Mirror

Harrow didn't realize—as her mind was still in shock, confused with the apparent impossible knowledge this woman possessed—that Legacy had been holding her hand, tugging her along the whole way to the elevators and down the hallways to her hotel room in the Palazzo. When they arrived at the door, the stranger let go of her, and she wasn't sure whether to be grateful or annoyed. Instead, she stood motionless, her gaze still glazed and mouth still slightly agape, as the woman who had somehow identified her opened the door into the exceptional Las Vegas suite.

She held the door for Harrow, allowing her to step into the entry. She looked all around the room, forgetting to hear the sound of the door being closed behind her.

The nearly two-thousand square-foot Lago Suite was one of the somewhat higher-class rooms the resort had to offer. She stepped in to see a small counter and bar directly in front of her. There was no evidence it had been used, except for the several large shopping bags set upon it, evidently from her host's previous trip to the Shoppes and other resort malls. On her right was a pool table, lit only by the sunshine spilling into the room from the enormous window which dominated the far wall. To her left was a door into a small kitchen area, complete with doors leading out to a balcony. Another door stood across the room from her, and through its crack Harrow could see the foot of a bed, already having been made up by the housekeeping staff.

Legacy stepped in front of her guest, not being careful at all in keeping their arms from brushing together as she passed by. Her swinging hips led Harrow over to the seating area by the large window to the right. Harrow looked at the pool table as she passed, noting that only the eight and cue balls were out of the pockets.

She took a seat on the couch, leaning back to keep the sunlight on her left from invading her eyes. Her host pulled out one of the golden-beige velvety chairs from the table in the corner, sitting backwards in it such that her chin rested on the chair's head. From this position, it looked to Harrow as though she was wearing nothing at all, as her crossed arms had no clothing on them, and the chair concealed the straps on her shoulders.

"So how did a Telignen end up on Earth? Actually, scratch that; how did you get off Peplorix?"

"Uhm, well I—" Harrow attempted to start, before being cut off by the apparently unfinished woman.

"Cause I thought—and maybe I'm wrong, it's been a while since I was out there—that no one could get on or off-world, at all. Like it was literally a crime on par with treason to abandon planet. Is the war over?"

"I really—"

"I mean, that would really be a surprise." Legacy continued, interrupting her attempt to explain herself again. "You guys have been fighting since I was an infant, I thought. I guess everything has to end at some point, right?"

"I have no idea what you're talking about." Harrow tried to say firmly. She felt strangely guilty being so direct, even though she'd been exactly that all her life. Well, all her life that she chose to be Lady Harrow.

"Oh don't be coy, hun. I recognized that dust with the money back there. I may not have ever met a Telignen, but I know *humans* can't do that. I know an *alien* when I see one."

"Yes, I—" Harrow tried to start, catching herself. She had no reason to open up about this; she could walk right out the door right now. But, somehow, she didn't want to. Even though she did. But the urge to do so was fading. She was relaxing, getting more comfortable. She started over. "I *am* a Telignen. But I don't remember Peplorix at all. I don't know anything about it, or about any kind of war. My parents brought me here when I was born; to protect me, they said.

"But they only told me that when I was seventeen. Before that, as far as I knew, I was human. I felt betrayed and angry and scared. So I ran away, fended for myself, learned my powers myself. I never looked back, and never asked about any of it. I know less than you do, apparently."

"Oh damn, those stories I heard must be true then. I didn't think they could be, but wow; that makes a lot of sense now." the stranger said, not making it clear whether she was trying to be vague or not as she became lost in thought.

"What stories? How do you know so much?"

"You think you're the only alien on Earth?" Legacy said condescendingly, though clearly intending to invoke camaraderie—which worked. "I'm a Svuarti."

"*Sfoo-are-dee*?" Harrow asked, trying to learn the pronunciation as well as the meaning.

"Yeah, you got it."

"What's that?"

"Wow, they didn't tell you a damn thing, did they?" Legacy asked, slightly annoyed. Lady Harrow hoped it was more frustration with her parents than with her. She wasn't sure, however, why she hoped that. These feelings were unfamiliar. Much like the knowledge currently being imparted on her. "So Svuarti are this species from... I don't actually know what planet we're from. They've always been big on travelling, ever since they mastered space travel. I was born in a merchant colony on Yufulyiv."

Harrow remained silent, hoping to make it clear that she didn't have any idea what Legacy was talking about or what any of the proper nouns were supposed to mean.

"Ok, let me try again. Hi, I'm Legacy. I'm from a species of trade-obsessed aliens called Svuarti, who can sense the sentimental value of people, places, and things. They live in colonies on dozens of planets, but mostly are nomadic space travelers. I was born on a planet called Yufulyiv, and when I accidentally came to Earth to make a deal with some shady-types, decided to stick around.

"Turns out, humans are really primitive, and Svuarti can influence them to a certain extent if we're touching something sentimental to them. So I live like a secret queen here, instead of struggle to make deals out there in the trade routes."

This whole situation was overwhelming Lady Harrow. With each sentence, she found herself tucking her legs and arms up and in further and further, until she resembled a crying child, though her eyes remained fixed on the storyteller, her mind eager to lap up all of this information that she barely understood. She'd been among humans for too long.

"I can't believe I actually found another alien woman on Earth. I can't describe how I feel right now, this is just... surreal." was all Harrow was able to get out.

"I know; crazy serendipity. But seriously, back to you. I know you don't know anything about it, but I just need to think out loud for a second cause this is nuts.

"So Peplorix has been closed for, let's see—I'm seventy-four Yufulyiv years old, that's... forty-six Earth years or so—about forty years, I think. Civil war; every Telignen on the planet was enlisted on one side or the other. Had to fight. Or so I'm told."

"Why were they fighting?"

"No idea. Never asked, never came up. Probably something dumb, if they even remember it, but neither side would give in. Defecting was unheard of, and there was so much strife and conflict no one could get in the planet safely because the other side would see it as a threat. Most dangerous place for traders, historians, and explorers in civilized space. And because of that, there were rumors—stories, that I always figured were old spacefarer's superstitions—that a child hadn't been born on Peplorix since before the war began. But if your parents left when you were born... Maybe they really were protecting you. Maybe they defected rather than let you come into a world like that."

"Oh, I... I had never thought about that." Lady Harrow felt a knot of guilt for having abandoned her parents all those years ago. But it was fleeting. They should still have told her sooner, brought her up better. Protected her from the nightmares.

32

She thought to ask another question of Legacy, despite her imperfect knowledge, but the woman beat her to it.

"So they named you Lady Harrow?"

"Oh, ah— No. No, I picked that name when I ran away. I don't use my birth name anymore. As far as I'm concerned it's a lie. I may not be human, but I'm not Telignen either. Not theirs, anyway."

"I gotcha. Same here, I don't use my birth name. Legacy just sounded cool given what I can do to humans."

The two alien women sat in silence for a moment, sizing each other up further in each other's eyes.

After what seemed like several minutes, Legacy broke the silence.

"I want to show you something. Come on, you'll love it."

"What, now? Where?" Harrow said as she grabbed Legacy's outstretched hand, who had already risen from her seat and offered it. This was moving quickly, and Harrow was unsure she should be as calm as she inexplicably felt.

She pulled her to her feet. Their arms brushed together again as their faces nearly met, but Legacy turned quickly—not out of shyness, but to lead Harrow back to the door. "You'll see; I promise you won't be disappointed." she assured the Telignen as her hand twisted the door handle, pulling it swiftly for the pair to walk back through.

It was 9:13 before the sky began to turn from a cool navy to a haunting black. It was a much different experience to see the sun fall so slowly from way out in the desert. Behind them, Harrow could see the faint brightness of Las Vegas on the horizon, invading on the perfect darkness at the very west edge of their field of vision.

She turned her eyes back to the road, back to the section of sky that was still grasping at the smallest strings of daylight fading behind the mountains. There weren't many other cars out here, so Legacy was being a little more reckless with her driving than one would normally be. In part to amuse her passenger, she guessed, as it was a dull trip.

Lady Harrow's skepticism had vanished once she'd gotten in her new ally's truck. She was fully invested in Legacy—in what she had to offer as a source of knowledge and understanding, and as a companion. A partner in crime. A friend she could be wholly forthcoming with.

So she sat patiently on the Svuarti's mysterious car ride to nowhere.

As her eyelids began to fail her, Harrow felt the vehicle pull onto the shoulder of the desert road and begin to slow down. After a few moments, it turned more sharply off the road, driving carefully over the rough brush and gravel of the Nevada wasteland, before coming to a complete stop.

They stepped out of the vehicle—a very nice, seemingly brand new, silver pickup truck. It looked to have all the high-end amenities in it from what Harrow could see, in addition to being large and versatile. Perfectly built for just this sort of excursion and then some.

Legacy came around to the back of the truck, and Lady Harrow followed her footsteps on her side. When she opened the trunk door and hopped on, the Telignen looked up in confusion, though with a coy smile betraying the rest of her face.

"Where are we? What are we doing here?"

"Just get up here, *m'lady.*" Legacy teased, stretching out her hand once again to help her passenger up into the back of the truck, the headlights of which now turned off in disuse.

A few pillows and blankets were already in the back with them; they appeared to have been folded previously, but were knocked about some by the driving and rough terrain. Legacy grabbed two of the pillows and set them side by side, resting her head on one. She let her chest rise with a sigh as invitation for Harrow to do the same. She followed suit, but angled herself to look at Legacy rather than the sky, as the Svuarti was.

"Okay, I'm here. What did you want to show me?"

Legacy didn't respond, but rather lifted her arm up, angled somewhat over Harrow and straight up into the blackened sky. Harrow's gaze followed the dark arm's flesh up to the hand, which she could now tell was shaped into a fist, but for one finger, pointing into the sky.

She turned her head to try and see where the finger was aimed at, but couldn't quite make it out. Legacy nudged her, and Harrow moved her head closer to Legacy's arm, above her face, with her hair streaming down onto the familiar stranger's neck. She used this new vantage to try and make out what she was supposed to be looking at.

All she saw were the stars. Granted, they were beautiful stars. She had never been able to see so many; the light pollution from Las Vegas always hid them all, and the few times she had been in darker portions of the city, she saw only a handful, barely flickering against the planet's atmosphere. Out here, she could see a staggering number.

It was still an imperfect visage, as from pictures she had seen from perfect positions on Earth, she knew that the stars made out the spectacular shape of the galaxy's arm in ideal conditions. This was far from a galactic quantity. It was still breathtaking, though.

However, there were stars all over the sky. Lady Harrow still couldn't tell what was special about where Legacy was pointing in particular.

"Alright, I give. What am I supposed to be seeing?" she begged her guide.

"That star right there—you see it just below that little cluster of three?"

"Yeah. It doesn't look any different than any of the other ones, but yeah, I see it."

"That's Peplorix's sun."

Lady Harrow's breathing stopped. She didn't know for how long.

"Right now," Legacy continued. "Your home planet is orbiting that star. Right now, probably, your people are fighting with each other, dying among each other, crying over each other, completely oblivious to everything happening outside of their little world. But, if we could look at it close-up with some impossibly perfect telescope, we wouldn't be able to see any Telignen. Your whole civilization, from our perspective, doesn't exist yet, and won't for, like, three hundred million years.

And if the people on your planet stopped fighting for long enough to use that same impossible telescope to look at us right now, from their perspective, they would see the things that lived before the dinosaurs."

Lady Harrow imagined that whatever Legacy was saying was inspirational and cosmically eye-opening. But she was still focused on the raw emotion of seeing even a glimmer of what was apparently her home. The star that kept warm the planet she was born on. The sun her parents had lived under, and fought under, and loved under. The system they fled to protect her from lifetimes of pain and war.

"That's amazing." was all she was able to muster. And yet it didn't even begin to describe how impressive it was, or how grateful she was for having been shown it.

Evidently, Legacy knew this, and recognized there were no words for her feelings at that moment. So instead, she laid one hand on Lady Harrow's cheek, pulling her face closer to kiss her. Not deeply, not especially passionately. But with care and intent.

"Thank you for showing me this." Lady Harrow said, breaking away from the familiar alien's face.

Legacy nodded, and then turned her head back to the sky, looking around in an apparent attempt to find something else. Her head and eyes darted about the web of stars seemingly independent of each other, seeking stellar landmarks to guide her to whatever she was looking for.

She must have found it, as her hand once again became a pointing finger, this time at a portion of sky just above the horizon to their right.

"See those four stars that are kinda almost in a row?" she asked her passenger.

"Uhm... Yes!" Harrow responded eagerly.

"The one on the far right; that's Yufulyiv's star."

"Wow, that's so much brighter!"

"It's much closer. If they looked at us right now, they would see the dinosaurs being choked by Earth's burning atmosphere."

The two looked on at the planet's sun with awe for some time.

Eventually—Harrow was finding it more and more difficult to keep track of time with Legacy—the Svuarti woman turned back to her, and they began to kiss again.

As Legacy's hand fell to Harrow's waist, resting on the side of her exposed stomach, she pulled away in pause.

"I've been meaning to ask: how do you look human?" Legacy put as delicately as Harrow would have known how.

"How do *you* look human?" Harrow responded, half-teasing.

"Genetic modification." she replied with a shrug. "I got my ship from a planet called Flavaphus. There're a hundred different aliens there, because whatever the original inhabitants were, they mastered genetic modification, so they just mess with themselves for fun. The technology's built into everything they do, like cup holders on Earth."

"Oh, wow. That's... interesting." Harrow said, a bit taken aback by the strangeness of other worlds. "My parents must have put some mental instructions in my head, 'cause there are some binds on my mind to constantly keep up an illusion of a human body over my Telignen one. They didn't even tell me *that*, I figured that out when I learned to start doing it to myself by examining their locks. I don't even know what I really look like. What I feel like."

"You can't break it? It sounds like you know how to."

"I could, except it's tied to a physical thing. And I don't know what the thing is, so I can't undo the threads."

Legacy thought for a moment. "Well, you'll always look like a Telignen to me. And you look..."

Lady Harrow didn't let her finish her thought. She grabbed her head again to pull her into her own kiss, and Legacy took the opportunity to climb on top of her new alien companion.

Harrow once again broke their contact.

"R'Bec." she said.

"Sorry?" her lover-apparent asked, unsure if she'd heard correctly.

"That's my birth name. R'Bec."

"*Rib-eck*. I like it." she replied, pecking the Telignen again. "Jieadea."

"*Ee-yaw-dee*?"

"Yep, that's *my* name."

"Okay. Hello, Jieadea." Lady Harrow said smiling.

"Greetings, R'Bec." Legacy replied, holding up her hand with her fingers pressed together to appear as only three.

The pair of alien women laughed, before returning to their unity under the light of their home suns, and the many other stars that shone on the Sonora Desert.

Issue 5
Worth Its Weight

The LVPD Narcotics Division was never known for their efficacy. They did their best, of course, and there were plenty of successes to count towards them. Even their failures were eclipsed by their high-profile arrests and record-breaking raids. However, no matter how many criminals were put behind bars or how big of a lab was put out of commission, it never seemed to make a dent in the city's vice problem. Not to Detective Colton Wallace's eyes, anyway.

Now, though, there was a change in the wind. The tides were turning in favor of justice. But he still wasn't satisfied, because the credit belonged neither to him, nor to his unit.

He strode into the precinct, stoic as ever. He always saw the gazes of his fellow officers, both those he worked with and those of other divisions, but was never one to let it change his behavior. Conversations ended abruptly as he passed. Breaths slowed or halted as eyes followed him down the hall. He was respected for his efficiency and persistence, and feared for his temper. Most didn't recognize that this anger was almost always directed inward. Humans made mistakes, but it was that very understanding that made him loathe when he did.

As he walked down the hall toward his destination, he caught the passing whispers of his coworkers.

"Got a guy in holding who thinks he saw some kinda monster."

"I heard something like that from my CI the other day."

"Funny, I can't get ahold of my informant. No one's seen him in a month."

These were not conversations Wallace wouldn't like to hear, but they hushed at his passing all the same.

Wallace entered the interrogation room that had been closed off for the past three weeks. His desk was neat and handsomely maintained, but it was far too small to contain the work he was doing. He couldn't well keep it on the computer, after all; if the organizations he was after found what he'd discovered, they'd scurry back into their rat holes and never come out.

Someone else was in the room, leaning against the plain metal table, looking at the wall to the right.

"Added anything?" he asked of the other officer.

"Nah, just looking for loose threads." he replied.

Officer Victor Levin was one of the few people fully read-in on Wallace's investigation. Naturally, much of the department was aware of his case and knew about it to one degree or another, and Captain Slieman had to be on board with every step, but Colton didn't trust anyone with it as much as he did Levin.

"Still can't believe it's been three weeks, with no sign of slowing down." Victor said.

"I can't believe it's *only* been three weeks. More progress than we've had in three decades." Wallace replied, joining his partner at the table to look at the cork board.

It depicted a web of destruction; case files for and theories regarding the recent collapse of one criminal organization or drug operation after another. Crime scene photos showed mob bosses and lab operators tied up and unconscious on the ground of their former headquarters. Evidence lists showed that the means of production and storage were kept and taken into police custody, but no substantial amount of product was being found; only enough to earn a conviction with. Memos were pinned to the board, detailing how even that product vanished from police custody, with full chain of possession logged and accounted for, only to go missing after the final step, in lockdown.

And at the center of it all, written confessions and interrogation notes, alluding to the perpetrator of this apparent vigilantism.

Two women: an enforcer and a supervisor of some sort. Apparently, the former was known among the criminal underworld as a representative of the mysterious Menteur, an up-and-coming supplier of hard substances. The other was an enigma all her own, even to those arrested individuals. Only the one identified as Lady Harrow carried a gun, but although the drug lords and gangsters all recalled quite clearly having been shot and wounded, none had anything more than a bruise.

The Detective was grateful that these two women were taking out big targets from the Narcotics Division's book, but the purpose was clear. They were stealing the product as well, and the Menteur was filling the power vacuum his representatives were creating. This was criminal warfare. And that made them just as guilty as the people they were allowing Wallace to arrest.

"Anything on the tip line?" he asked Officer Levin.

"Nothin'. The Menteur runs a tight operation."

"Nobody's perfect." Colton affirmed in a gruff.

"He's pretty damn close. And from what we've heard, so are his girls."

"What I don't get," the Detective said, switching subjects. "Is how they're taking these thugs out. They all agree; this 'Lady Harrow' has a gun. She's shooting it. She's hitting them. But they just end up with bruises you'd get from stubbing your toe. Where's the force? How are two petite women eliminating seasoned, hardened, muscled ex-cons? And making off with all that coke?"

Victor stayed silent. Wallace wasn't sure whether due to not having an answer, or politely recognizing that the question was rhetorical. Either way, he continued.

"Do we have a sketch yet?"

"Oh, that's right! I knew there was another reason I came in here." Victor exclaimed. He slid a manila folder from the table behind him along the metal and closer to him, taking out the paper inside. He stood up straight and stepped toward the corkboard, taking a pin to the page and positioning it above the descriptions of the suspects—right in the middle of the board.

"That's Lady Harrow. According to the sketch artist, anyway." the officer declared proudly.

It was Wallace's turn to stand up straight, as he too stepped toward the board, bringing his face inches from the artist's rendition of his nemesis. Lady Harrow: the woman who was taking his unit's glory, while also soiling that heroism with more crime and villainy.

She was Native American, judging by the facial structure. Her hair was long and flowing. Her skin was without blemish.

There wasn't much more that needed to be said; she was a woman. She was a criminal.

"Wait a second." Colton said. From the corner of his eye, he saw something. As if Harrow's face somehow whispered to him a new clue.

He backed up a bit to eye the small map of Las Vegas on the right side of the board. Marker had been used to denote where the hits were taking place, and the territories affected.

Wallace violently pulled the map off the wall, using as much of what remained of his patience to be careful not to rip it from its pins in the corners. He practically slammed the map onto the table, prompting Victor to turn around and look at it as well, to try and grasp what he had missed himself.

"All this time... We've been saying there's no pattern with these hits. The Menteur is taking out the competition indiscriminately—but what if he's not?"

"I don't get it, there isn't a pattern, and he is taking—"

"No, no you see, it makes sense now!" the Detective interrupted his officer. "Which group was taken out first?"

"The Irish. They had the smallest territory." Victor answered correctly.

Wallace took his own red marker out of his pocket and wrote a small number one beside the X denoting the headquarters' location. "Next?"

"The Chinese."

Again, Wallace marked the headquarters with a number two. "And then, what? The Italians?"

"No, they took out the lab at Bonanza and Lamb."

"Oh, yes. Then... the Winchester gang! And *then* the Italians." Colton wrote numbers three, four, and five respectively. They went further down the list, marking each hit that had been made in the past three weeks attributed to the Menteur's associates. Now, they had a clear map not only of where the skirmishes were taking place, but when. "Notice anything?"

"No. There's still no pattern. They're not hitting them from strongest to weakest, smallest to biggest, oldest to newest... It's random, there's nothing here."

"Oh no, there's definitely something. Consider the Chinese. They're some of the most organized and well-armed drug traffickers in Vegas. They took 'em out. They're also going for small fries like the random street dealers. Even the Winchesters; middle of the road. No one's safe."

"Yeah, we know this, Colton."

"Who are they *not* hitting?"

Victor paused. "Oh."

"*Yeah*. We've established they can hit whoever they want. Eight operations, no matter the odds against them. But there's a very clear hole. An obvious hole that they could very easily take out—hell, that would be in order geographically—that they are intentionally not filling in. Right..." Wallace put his finger on the map. "Here."

The Detective's finger pressed against the heavy glossy paper. Above it was the 515. To the southwest was the Strip. The territory was well known, as any other gang's territory would be.

"The Del Toros. He's in league with them." Colton declared.

Officer Levin stood in the bare high-class apartment, looking around with his hands on his hips. He was trying to make sense of this, and getting nowhere.

The Menteur's women, Lady Harrow and the other, had struck again. Despite the Detective's realization three days ago, the two—indeed, the whole division—had made no progress in finding them or putting a stop to them. Stings took time to organize, and needed concrete details to legally put into motion. So all they could do was wait. And if Victor had learned anything in his time in Narcotics, it was that Detective Wallace was not a patient man.

"Same story as ever, here. Damnit!" he heard Wallace say as he walked into the apartment's main room. Evidently he'd just finished searching the bedroom. "No drugs. Just what was on the Russians. Enough to convict—and evidence that more was here—but it's all gone now."

"Fingerprints?" Victor tried to ask delicately, already knowing the answer, but trying to be productive anyway.

"None. As usual. Like they're ghosts."

This was the closest the pair had ever been to the women. They had left only a few hours ago; it was the same night. They swiftly subdued the Russian leadership and made off with effectively all of their supply here. Naturally, as a major organized syndicate, they were bound to have more stashed away. But as with the Irish, and the Winchesters, it would be gone by morning. Leaving them no closer to finding the would-be vigilantes or their employer, who would take up the role of distributor in the area, now.

"If we stake out the Del Toros—"

"Don't even try, kid." Levin's superior replied with a sigh. "I already asked Slieman. It's a no-go. 'Just a hunch.' He won't allow it."

Victor felt for Colton. He knew the Detective only wanted to clean up the city. He didn't mind that someone else was doing it; he minded that it was for the wrong reasons.

Wallace clicked his fingers, looking up. "I've got an idea! 'Nother hunch. Meet me in the car." He quickly skirted out of the room, his hands behind his back as his eyes looked to the floor, deep in thought. Victor followed from a safe distance.

When they got to Wallace's car—an unmarked Detective's vehicle, necessary for a Narcotics official—he took his seat behind the steering wheel. Officer Levin sat in the passenger seat, where he waited in silence. The Detective was often one to mull things over before making a clear announcement, to ensure he would get all of his details right the first time.

"Who's left?" he asked abruptly.

"Sorry?" Victor asked, unsure what his superior meant.

"Gangs, mobs, crime groups. Who's left?" Wallace specified. His eyes were fixed on the steering wheel of the car, still yet to be started.

"Oh, um... I think just the Westside Crew and the Sons of Washington, plus a few smaller crowds north of the 215, though they haven't gone that far north so they may not consider them a problem. That's not including the independent dealers though, and who knows how many labs."

"The last two major groups standing against the Del Toros… One of them is going down next. We need to be there when they do."

"How do we figure out which one?"

"We don't." Colton replied, turning his head now to face his associate. "We'll have to guess. Hope for the best. And if we're wrong, we stay put and wait some more, cause then they'll be the very last."

"So a stakeout, then?"

Detective Wallace nodded. "But off the books. It's a wild theory; a baseless plan. But it'll work. We were so close this time! We can do better. We will be better. It's time to meet the ghosts, face to face."

Colton's eyes were fixed on the building—a golf supply store on the west side of the city. The concept was a popular business venture, given the number of golf courses and country clubs in the western United States. This establishment had been long suspected of being the Westside Crew headquarters by the LVPD, despite its size. Naturally, if correct, it wasn't being used for storage or manufacturing; only dealing, laundering, and sales tracking. However, organizing sting operations took time and resources, both of which were hard to come by, especially without preexisting evidence.

Detective Wallace and Officer Levin were not here to take down the notorious upper-society drug traffickers, though. Indeed, Wallace secretly hoped they could catch their true targets after they finished with the gangsters themselves.

The Detective had been meticulous in planning this night, and if he was correct, so too had Lady Harrow and her mysterious cohort. In twenty-one days, the women had exacted nine attacks on other criminal operations. That was one strike every two-to-three days. It had so far been two days since the Russians had been taken out, and as it was a Saturday, this golf supplier was open until midnight—an unusual business practice for the industry, further alluding to the shady dealings going on there. It was therefore an ideal climate for the Menteur's enforcers to make an attempt on this yet-another rival.

"Time?" Wallace asked, unwilling to take his gaze away from the lit storefront for even long enough to glance at his dashboard.

"11:09." Levin replied. Wallace heard him sip the last drops from his large soda, eagerly and anxiously scrounging for what little contents remained. The sound prompted him to reach again for his own drink, which was only half empty.

They had been there for nearly three-and-a-half hours. The Detective didn't expect their marks to arrive until nearly closing time—if even at all—but he wanted to be sure his bases were covered, and his closest confidant didn't mind. So they continued their watch, having finished their meal and snacks. For Victor's sake, Colton hoped this didn't take too much longer; he had no interest in sharing the rest of his beverage.

Finally, his patient vigilance was rewarded. Approaching from the right, along the other closed stores of the open strip mall, were the two women. It was dark, but the same features from the police sketches were still discernible.

"There they are!" Officer Levin said excitedly, pressing his outstretched finger against the windshield. "What's the plan?"

"We wait for them to go in," Wallace began. "Hang back for a few minutes to let the situation simmer—and so we have something to arrest them for—then burst in. 'You're under arrest for racketeering and drug trafficking.' Read 'em their Mirandas, book 'em. Smooth and clean."

The Officer nodded, sitting back in the passenger seat to wait for the signal. He instinctively reached for his paper cup and attempted to take another sip from its straw, but caught only air, having forgotten he had just finished it off moments ago.

Wallace too reached for his soda, but put it down quickly when he heard a loud pop from in front of them. He turned to Levin, his hand already on the door handle.

The two policemen ran towards the glass storefront, hands disciplined on their firearms. They each pressed their backs against the pillars on either side of the establishment. Wallace made a hand motion to Levin, before moving in with the Officer on his rear.

Colton pushed the glass door in, weapon trained to the counter. Lady Harrow was in a stand-off with two men behind the register, four guns between them. The other woman was back some, in the middle of the floor.

"LVPD, drop your weapons!" the Detective shouted. The mystery woman turned quickly, raising her arms up—though not very convincingly.

Lady Harrow turned her head, then took the opportunity to turn her unusually large-barreled pistols in her hands with terrifying grace, hitting her opponents in the face with the butts of her guns. She dropped them as her whole body turned toward the two cops.

51

"Lady Harrow, put your hands up. You're under arrest." Officer Levin said with a firm calmness that can only be learned from countless dangerous arrests.

The red-haired Native American woman did as instructed—though like her darker counterpart, without much conviction—letting her hands reach the level of her eyes. Once they did, she looked just past the two men and pointed right beside them with a single, casual finger.

Wallace glanced in that direction just in time to see several large golf clubs fall to the ground. He leapt back in surprise, avoiding being hit by the hard metal.

When he looked back up, Lady Harrow and the other woman had turned around, and were making way for the back room.

Victor sprang into action, leaping over the clubs to give chase. Lady Harrow turned as she ran through the door and gestured at the ground with her hand, as though wading through some invisible force.

When the Officer's feet would have hit the ground, his landing was broken by a flood of golf balls. His heel hit one, which awkwardly rolled under him. He lost strength in his ankle, and his whole body went down—legs and arms battered and bruised by dozens of golf balls that had come from nowhere.

Colton tried to wade through the trap, but his haste was impaired such that when he reached the door, it was already closed and... padlocked?

How did they have time to lock the door so thoroughly? He shot at the padlock, attempting to break its hold on the door handle.

It wouldn't even scratch.

Failing that, he opted to take aim for the door itself, weakening its hinges with three decisive bullets, allowing him to kick it down completely without too much strain. But by the time he was able to step through the empty frame and into the back room, there was no sign of the suspects. The back door was ajar, but the two were nowhere in sight.

Wallace turned back to head inside, disappointedly abandoning his fool's errand to tend to the downed Officer. He carefully kneeled down beside Levin to help him to his feet.

"You alright, Vic?"

"Yeah, I'm good. Just got the wind knocked outta me. C'mon, let's go!" the Officer said, unwilling to admit defeat.

"Forget it, man. They're gone."

"How can you say that? They can't be too far, we can—"

"No, kid." the Detective interrupted. "I don't think chasing them is gonna work. We'll have to regroup, think of something else.

"We've seen them now, though. We know they're behind it; we know their game." Wallace tried to reassure his protégé.

"Yeah... Yeah, okay." Victor submitted. "Let's at least grab these two, though."

"Agreed."

The two policemen turned to the men behind the counter. They peeked over the glass case to find them unconscious on the floor. Somehow, though, they were also already zip tied with their hands behind their backs.

"What the…?" Levin said. But Wallace had lost focus. He looked at the ground behind him.

The golf balls were getting darker. He crouched down to get a closer look, and tried to pick one of them up. As his fingers pressed against the white surface, though, they crushed the sphere, coating his skin in a flaky black dust. He shook his hand, and it separated from the ridges of his fingers, fluttering through the air before disappearing altogether.

The other golf balls were also all collapsing in on themselves, becoming small piles of ash-like crumbs on the green carpet, which themselves dissolved into nothingness.

The golf clubs, too, began to melt away into the same crusty debris, hovering in the air for a few moments before being whisked away into void.

It was all an illusion—all of it. The clubs falling, the golf balls on the floor, the padlock even! Wallace looked at the door sitting crooked on the ground to see the hook of the lock fade into dark particles, as the whole mechanism wobbled off and onto the ground and dispersed into a cloud of dust, before it all vanished.

He looked to Officer Levin, who had jumped behind the counter to cuff the two criminals quickly, before the zip ties around their wrists exploded in a puff of faint smoke, stirring into the cold, still air.

"What the Hell was that, Colt?" Victor said. His eyes were filled with dread and concern.

"Something unique, Vic." Colton replied. "Something very unique, and something way out of our league."

Issue 6
Pretense

"Good to see you again, James."

"Wish I could say the same, *m'lady.*"

"Oh, don't be like that. What have I ever done to you?"

"Nothing yet, but word travels fast. I see your friend there, I've heard the rumors."

This was what Lady Harrow was afraid of. She knew they had been too explicit, too public, in their attacks. Legacy knew it too, but she didn't care. But now that she thought about it, Harrow didn't care either. They were doing a service. Legacy was helping her, showing her a new, faster way to achieve her goals.

"I don't know what you've been told, James. The Menteur just wants to renegotiate our arrangement. He's got big plans for expansion."

"Then why isn't he here? I see the writing on the wall, H. Your expansion doesn't include us. You're here to see to that." the Sons of Washington leader said. His face was less than a foot from hers. This was more of a negotiation than he understood. Or, maybe he did understand, and that's why he was playing along with her.

"Then why aren't you fighting?" she asked even as the tips of her fingers met his, their hands both pressed on opposite sides of the table. They were both doing the same thing; trying to out-swagger the other. James had his crew. Harrow had Legacy.

"I don't shoot first. And when I do, I don't shoot ladies first."

"Good thing I'm no lady, then."

"How's that?"

"A lady…" Harrow started to answer, trying very hard not to instinctively twirl her fingers as she summoned a simple illusion. "Would stab you in the front!"

At this, a bat slugged right into James' backside, then vanished into the air with a billowing crash of dust. He recoiled forward in shock and pain as Lady Harrow jumped onto the table, his head at her feet.

She stretched her arms out as she conjured her notorious—though completely imaginary—comedically large pistols, and began unloading their nonlethal rounds into the assembled enforcers of the Sons of Washington.

The two directly behind their assailed leader barely had time to get their own firearms in their hands before they were down, grasping at their chests to fill the holes and stop the bleeding. Naturally, Lady Harrow felt no pity for them, and no need to aid them; they were totally unharmed. Once they woke up from their eventual shock-induced nap, they would find only ruffled shirts and spoiled pride as their injuries.

The others in the room had a little more time to join the firefight. The two directly behind Harrow turned their attention not to her, but to the unarmed Legacy against the wall behind them.

However, Legacy—a crafty and agile Svuarti—was swift and nimble, effortlessly bending down and slinking under and around their initial shots. They were quick to take new aim, but she was quicker in her calculation and execution of just the right motions to keep them on their toes.

She reached them quickly as the battle began, and weaved around their bodies just enough to reach into the back of their pants and relieve them of their wallets. One might think it a petty move to pickpocket someone while being beset with bullets, but this was a tactical maneuver for one of her kind.

She opened one, being careful to still pay attention to their attempts to shoot her, and found what she was looking for. She held it firmly between her fingers; a picture of one of their daughters, folded and cut to fit in his wallet so she would always be with him. A poetic weapon against a blubbering human.

With something so sentimental of the young man's in her possession, he was hers. She suggested to him—silently, in his own mind and his own words—that he stop trying to kill the poor unarmed woman, and turn his attention to the horrible excuse for a person trying to murder her for no good reason.

He was only happy to change his mind for his daughter's corrupted memory, and let his arms drop lower, aiming his weapon at his associate's—his enemy's—foot. He pulled the trigger, and a howl pierced through the rest of the ear-splitting gunfire and breaking of glass and furniture.

Legacy stepped over to him calmly and thanked him for 'rescuing' her, before exchanging his wallet for his gun. She kept the photograph of course, not that he would notice. She simply suggested he not think about it, and so he didn't. And wouldn't.

Then she bashed him in the head with the butt of her new piece, before doing the same to his still-wailing partner.

Meanwhile, Lady Harrow was dispatching the rest of the assembled crew. She knew this last organization was going to be the hardest to extinguish. Not because they were the biggest—they weren't—or the most well-armed and well-trained—although they were—but because they were the last. They had the most time to figure out what was going on and to prepare for it. Eight veterans of both the military and the criminal underworld, plus a former-spec-ops officer at the helm, with enough foresight, was a dangerous force indeed. But they did have one fault that Harrow and Legacy could extort.

They were human.

With the two men in front of her subdued, and James still recovering from the now-dissipated bat, the only ones standing against her now were the four armed mercenaries beside her, at the edges of the room. They had the advantage, any strategist and statistician could see that. But they were still human. Easy to exploit and confuse.

After stopping their fire with small corks at the ends of their barrels—invisible from their perspectives, they were simple illusions that dissolved the real bullets on contact, as long as Harrow could hold her focus—she let them believe they were still firing at her, and missing with rounds she was imagining flying past her. They began to move closer, allowing even her fictional bullet streams to grow tighter around her, and she knew this was where she had to take a chance.

Unable to focus enough to add any more illusions without releasing her hold on the corks currently keeping her safe, she could only move and manipulate the manifestations already present. She willed her corks to press against the edges of the men's weapons, inexplicably pulling them and adjusting the angles of the barrels and their arms.

What were also being adjusted, with very careful effort, were the lines of fire Harrow was willing to continue whistling through the air, despite noticing from their faces and relaxed fingers that none of the men were still pulling their triggers, and were probably out of real ammo by now. As their guns turned toward the men opposite them, the imaginary bullets sprayed closer and closer to their faces, grazing their cheeks. Finally, in all four of their confusion, the belief that a single round had penetrated their forehead—when in fact they had simply vanished with a puff of black smoke—caused the enforcers' brains to force their bodies to recoil in horror and pain.

Legacy had handled her two, and Harrow had single-handedly subdued—and from James' perspective, killed—six more of his finest Sons of Washington.

He put his hands up, still bending over slightly with the imagined pain of his initial assault.

Lady Harrow summoned another of her infamous pistols, and pressed it squarely against his head. She intended to let him believe he'd been shot and killed; to let him wake up in a few hours with metal cuffs around his wrists and iron bars at the edge of his blurred vision.

"Kill him, H." Legacy said with a concise tone.

"I plan to."

"No, *really* do it." Her voice was sharp and cruel, yet somehow still melodic and attractive to the illusionist's ears. "Show him what you are. Show me what you can do."

Any other day, Harrow wouldn't have listened to such a request. She would have thought about it for hours—over a few seconds—but would always come out right. She'd always be torn, but say no. Today, though, another part of her nagged in her head. Maybe it was a good idea to kill him.

No. It was pointless. It wouldn't further her goals any more than keeping him alive. It defeated the purpose of her plan and dropped her to the level of her foes.

And yet, it sounded so simple. So clean. A part of her that she didn't know existed was winning out. The debate was uneven, her conscience had the logic.

But something else inside of her claimed victory.

She pulled on the trigger she imagined for herself. She wished for the dust in the air to take the form of a bullet of lead in her weapon's barrel that wasn't really there. She allowed the illusion to continue to exist, even as it bore through the skin of James' forehead. She forced it to continue sliding through his skull, drilling a hole in his head, leaving a trail of fictional debris. She wanted it to tunnel through his brain—a bullet made of pretend, causing very real damage to the defenseless man's life. She would create lasting change with only the power of her mind.

Her imagination slowed down the events she willed to transpire, but the whole thing took less than a second to execute.

James was dead. He was really and actually dead.

As he fell—as his eyes rolled into his head, as if to look at the hole in his flesh between his eyes; as his legs gave out, letting him drop to his knees; as his face fell forward, prompting Lady Harrow to step back so as not to get blood on herself; as his brain matter erupted pitifully from the back of his cranium when his

60

face hit the floor—Lady Harrow thought long and hard about what she'd just achieved; what she'd just accomplished.

All of this lasted for hours, but passed in only a few seconds.

And then she broke.

Lady Harrow, too, fell to her knees. Her face, too, hit the ground; not out of lack of strength, but out of shock and regret.

She'd just killed someone.

A human, yes, but a living, sentient person.

Legacy approached from behind to congratulate her, and to console her.

"It's okay, H. You didn't have a choice. Hey. Hush now, it's okay. I've got you." the woman—her lover—said, as she reached her arms under Harrow and helped to lift the shattered Telignen to her feet.

"I don't— I can't— I... Have to go. I can't do this now. I—" Harrow tried to get out between sobs and sniffs. Her eyes were like fire, melting away her pride and confidence into tears. She tried to hold onto them, to keep them from streaming down her face, as she ran out of the small refitted parking garage. She didn't know where she was going, but she needed to get away. Away from what she had done.

Issue 7
Say the Word

"Harrow, wait!" Legacy shouted to her partner, who was running a few dozen feet away. It was late at night, and no one was around. There was no way she couldn't hear her.

But Lady Harrow didn't care. She kept on running, on and on, despite the protests of the only woman she considered a friend and ally on this awful rock. She ran along empty sidewalks and across dark streets, ignorant of her surroundings due to the tears welling from her eyes.

But she didn't care. Even having no concept of what was around her, or of where she was, she kept running. She wasn't thinking clearly. She wasn't thinking at all. Not about what she was even running from, or where she was running to. Not about who was chasing her, or why. She just let herself go on, hoping she'd find the answer to the questions she was refusing to ask herself.

Harrow was growing tired, though. She could run for longer than a human, but even Telignen bodies have their limits. She was starting to slow down.

But she didn't care. She would run to her very last breath, until her heart and her legs gave way. She would run to the moon and back, screaming and wheezing the whole time if it meant escape.

But it wouldn't do any good, because she couldn't run from this. For even as much as she refused to think about it, as much as she couldn't dare to admit it, she was running from herself. From what she had done, from what had happened to her that would allow her to do such a thing. It was her own intrusive self-loathing and regret that she was trying to flee, and it wasn't going to work.

But she didn't—

"Harrow, stop! Listen to me!"

As she was slowing down, Legacy was getting the opportunity to catch up. She was nearly at arm's reach now. Not thinking, and even without comprehension as to why, she turned a sharp left to duck down an alleyway. She didn't know where she was or how much further she could go, but she was determined to see her fruitless escape through.

She felt a hand on her shoulder. As if that was all that she needed, as if that was the final straw, she stopped. Her knees trembled as she continued to sob, even in the dry air of the summer night. After a moment, they gave out, and Harrow felt two hands upon her shoulders. She still couldn't see clearly, but was able to tell that there was no shape in front of her. Legacy was behind her. She always would be there for her.

From the rustling of cloth and change in pressure upon her, she could tell that Legacy kneeled down on the ground, too. Still beside her, unwavering in her concern.

"Shh..." the Svuarti whispered gently against the back of Harrow's head. "It's okay, H. I'm here for you. I've got you. We're all okay."

"I— I can't— I just—"

"I know. I know, trust me. Don't worry about it, you did the right thing. You did what you had to do."

The two aliens sat alone in the alley, ensnared by darkness, for what felt like hours. Over the next few minutes, Lady Harrow slowly regained her full awareness, and began to recover from her blubbering. In that silence, in which Legacy more tightly held her partner around her chest in concerned embrace, Harrow thought long and hard about what had happened, and what to say. She needed to talk about it. And she would.

Noticing that her weeping had been reduced to the occasional sniffle, and feeling that she was no longer shaking, Legacy took the opportunity and spoke first. "You ready to talk about it?"

Harrow nodded.

"Alright. What are you feeling?"

"Re— Regret. Fear."

"What are you afraid of?" Legacy asked as she shuffled around and in front of her lover to face her properly.

"Myself. What I just did. Whether I'll do it again."

"That's nothing to be scared of, R'Bec." Legacy said. Lady Harrow's eyes jumped at the use of her birth name. She looked at Legacy with a silent fury, but relaxed upon seeing her own eyes. The face in front of her was sincere and compassionate.

"Well I am, okay? I've never... I don't ever want to do that. That's what I told myself. It's just so—"

"Necessary, sometimes." Legacy finished for her. Her face still held warmth, but was more firm, now. "Some people—some creatures—don't get to live. It's natural. It's right. There are a ridiculous number of species in the universe, and not all of them are equal. That doesn't mean any are lesser; they're not. We're all important. But some of us are important because we have to die, some day. And some sooner than others. Don't mourn the dead, and don't hate yourself for being alive."

"The dead..." For some reason, Lady Harrow's mind had a hard time letting go of those two words. They stuck with her, and mulled around in her brain, bouncing off of synapses, as she tried to understand why her subconscious thought they were important.

"Yeah, just let him go. We're still here, and we're doing good work."

"Are we?" Harrow suddenly summoned the nerve to ask. She didn't mean to sound accusing, but such a question is hard to phrase with any tone besides defiance.

Legacy seemed taken aback, but tried to answer in the same smooth whisper she had been using to help calm Harrow. "We're doing what you wanted, aren't we? The Del Toros have nearly total control of the city's drug trade, and it's all filled with your fake stuff."

"But, that's not why we started working together." Harrow said before thinking. Although, she was thinking. More clearly now than she had in several days. "*The dead*. The zombies. *That's* why you found me, but we haven't done *anything* with them at all!"

Legacy put her hands on Lady Harrow's cheeks as she looked at her with clear love and concern. However, it was hard for Harrow to read from her face exactly what the Svuarti was concerned about.

"We haven't been finding any information on them. We don't know where to start. Better to focus on what we know we can change and improve, rather than chasing ghosts."

"They're not ghosts, Jieadea! They're real, and they're terrorizing the city from the shadows. If we don't know where to start then we should be trying to find out, not going in guns-blazing on the criminal underworld—which, by the way, I had a plan for that was being executed perfectly well!" Harrow was struggling to maintain her composure. Legacy was her partner, lover, and friend. But right now she was talking like they were on different sides, trying to solve two different problems.

Legacy looked at her deeply for several seconds. It seemed to Harrow that she was sizing her up, trying to gauge how serious she was about all of this. And she was very serious.

Finally, she spoke up. "Alright. I'm sorry I wasn't listening, but you're right. The drugs can wait—we're at a good place to pause anyway, the Del Toros can fill in the power vacuums and stabilize their new territory in the meantime. Let's figure out how to deal with those monsters."

Lady Harrow perked up with glee. She hugged Legacy earnestly, happy they came to an agreement. She let go, and the two stood up. Harrow reached for her back pocket to touch her lucky charm—just for a moment, just to remind her that she was safe and on the right track—but Legacy grabbed her hand and squeezed it, taking it up to her face and caressing it. She didn't need to feel the globe to know that she was loved.

Legacy pulled out her smart phone to figure out exactly where they were, and to find directions back to their now-shared studio home behind the graffiti-adorned brick wall.

Issue 8
Curse the Day

Kicks didn't hate going to Mass nearly as much as usual. Ordinarily, his grandmother would drag him along, being the God-fearing Mexican woman that she was. He would come along without complaint, of course, because it was important to her, and she was the only family he had left. But most days, he didn't really pay much attention to the sermons or readings.

It wasn't that he didn't believe in God. He just never got the sense that God believed in him. He tried to do good, to live by the words of Jesus as best he could. But, he was a member of a gang and drug ring, so he presumed his continued faith would never be rewarded. But what choice did he have?

Just as he loved his grandmother enough to go to church with her every Sunday, he loved her enough to want to protect her however he could. And it was an unfortunate fact that she lived in the Del Toros' territory. It was a dangerous place for such an old woman; even if no one was going to target her, skirmishes between other local crime groups were plentiful enough that she could get caught up in the crossfire. At least if he was involved with them, he could try to keep things away from her, or have better resources with which to protect her. That's all he wanted.

Whether the Lord would look favorably on his intentions over his actions or not, Kicks kept up with what he was doing anyway. But there was more reason to join his grandmother today than just out of respect for her.

The zombies.

The stories started becoming more frequent over the last few weeks. Told in hushed whispers in the early morning, as far from their nocturnal hours as possible, the tales of those decaying monsters with abyssal eyes were casting a shadow of fear—and not just over the Del Toros. All of Las Vegas was cowering from the ghouls that weren't quite there. Kicks wasn't sure what to believe, but most of the reports from his friends and associates lined up pretty well with each other. And of course, there was the creature he had seen.

And that was why he was with the Del Toros. It was on his grandmother's *street*. It was at her *house*! It hobbled along the road for some unknown purpose. If the other accounts were to be believed, it was looking for something. Scavenging. But what could it want from such a poor neighborhood?

He was afraid to admit that he didn't know. He was scared of what the horrible answer might be. So, Kicks went to Mass with a skip in his step and a breath held in his lungs, hoping for some divine intervention; some guidance and courage in this trying time.

If there was going to be any help from on-high, though, it wasn't immediate. Kicks and his grandmother walked out of the temple and drove back home just the same as always.

"Alright *abuela*, need me to get you anything?" he asked, helping his grandmother get settled on her living room couch.

"Oh no, *miho*. You go have fun, I'll be fine."

"You sure? I don't have to go out, the guys'll understand."

"You do not have to worry about me so much. Go, go! The only thing I'm scared of is whether Juan will believe Carmelita in my stories." she said, laughing as she turned on her television and navigated to her recorded soap operas.

"Okay, I'll see you tonight. Love you!"

"I love you, sweet boy. Have fun and make good choices."

Those last few words stung, but he didn't let it show. Kicks stepped out the front door and started down the sidewalk, shame painting his face, knowing he was letting his grandmother down every day. But he swallowed his pride, because he knew it was all for her.

It was a bright day in Las Vegas, and people were taking advantage of the tolerable late-summer temperature. People were walking to the grocery store, jogging or biking to work, and a few kids were even playing on the sidewalk.

Granted, most of this wasn't out of the ordinary where Kicks lived. This area was so ripe with crime because the conditions here fostered it. The neighborhood was poor, but that wasn't a direct cause of the tension. No, it was only another symptom of the real problem: most of the community was Latino.

Kicks could go on and on about his thoughts on why that meant most of the people he knew didn't have a decent car, or struggled to feed their kids. He could get lost in his head thinking about where they'd gone wrong, about when the country became so irresponsible in its treatment of so many Americans. There were a lot of flaws—a laundry list of issues that brought him to where he was. Key among them, though, was simply that people didn't care enough. Not just about racism or the broken economy; people forgot how to care about other people. How to consider what others are going through, and not just acknowledge it, but empathize with them, and feel empowered to take their hand and stand with them. That was how he saw it all, anyway.

Having been thinking too hard, Kicks didn't realize he was about to walk right into someone—until they were both already on the ground.

He stood up, rubbing his tail bone as he recollected himself.

"Yo, I'm so sorry man. Are you okay?" Kicks asked with genuine concern.

The man he'd knocked over was still sitting on the sidewalk. Kicks reached his arm out to help him to his feet.

"Yeah man, I'm alright. Thanks." he replied.

The stranger, now standing upright, looked about six-one or six-two. He had some of the smoothest dark skin Kicks had ever seen—it hardly even reflected the sunlight on the cloudless day. He wore a red muscle shirt and baggy cargo pants. His baseball cap was haphazardly set backwards on his short, curly hair.

As Kicks looked him over, his eyes caught on the man's feet.

"Oh man, check out those sweet kicks!" he said excitedly.

"Oh yeah, you like 'em? Brand new, just got 'em Friday." he replied. His voice was deep, but soothing. He could be a voice actor, or even a weatherman.

The man was wearing a pair of bright yellow Nike Air Max 97s. The design had been around for twenty-one years in some form or another—based on the bullet trains of Japan, they used a mix of leather, foam, and naturally, Nike Air. However, the new yellow colorway had only just released this month, clocking in at one-hundred and sixty dollars.

"Man, those look sweet. Congrats!"

"Thanks lil dude. Peace." The stranger smiled politely before continuing on his way. Kicks stayed in place for a few more seconds, awestruck with how impressive they looked, even despite the gaudy color.

He looked down at his own pair of white-and-grey Adidas Duramo 9s, a few years too old. They weren't overly fancy shoes, but Kicks didn't have the money to spend a fortune when he could only afford one pair for all occasions, and running was universal. They were soft and comfy—or they were when he got them; now they just felt like any other sole—and made with breathable mesh. A not-uncommon design for athletic footwear, but important features nonetheless.

But he was wasting time. He needed to meet up with his buddies.

Most people didn't understand what drew honest people to join criminal groups. Kicks got no rush from aiding the Del Toros in their illicit activities, even if he was only a lookout, for the most part. But the Mexican gang, like many others, provided more than drugs to the community they claimed as territory. In a strange sort of way, they provided safety. While firefights between rival organizations did occur, many gangs—especially those born in lower-class neighborhoods of minorities—reimplemented some level of justice into the local systems. The Del Toros, for example, were actively charitable to the less fortunate of their own, and offered some protections from prejudiced police, if only by drawing their attentions to them rather than the innocents.

And to Kicks, the drug ring provided a new sense of family. His grandmother was all he had, and although she was a beacon of love and support for her only grandson, he yearned for some level of fraternity. Of belonging.

71

He was going to meet and hang out with some of the others from the Del Toros, now. His position at the Laundromat—keeping an eye out for Jenna for thieves and other enforcers—was effectively a job, so although he was expected to be active within the group at nearly all times, he had his days off from that role. So, today he was looking forward to hanging out at the local bowling alley. He wasn't very good, but it was something to do, and he did enjoy the company of the some of the other guys.

When Kicks arrived, he peered down the row of lanes and respective seating areas for his party. There were a few other families part way through their games, but it looked like his friends had yet to arrive.

Not wanting to waste their bowling time waiting for them, he walked over to the small arcade. It wasn't as extensive or exciting as those at some of the larger bowling alleys, or even dedicated arcades that he'd passed by. There were only a dozen games, mostly simple video racing or instant-prize machines.

Kicks wasn't really a fan of racing games, though. The scissor machine—where one attempts to cut a very strong cord with some very weak blades controlled by a finnicky joystick—was definitely out. He liked to think he was pretty good at the back-and-forth stacking game, but it didn't look like there were any good prizes.

Since none of the arcade machines looked particularly fun or easy enough, he chose the one with the biggest potential prize payout: a crane machine containing a brand-name smartwatch.

Naturally, Kicks was all-too-familiar with the trick of crane machines. While they did require some level of skill in placement of the arm and even the swing of the claw to ensure the fingers reached around and under the desired object, that skill was only rewarded when combined with exceptional luck. It was well-documented that settings inside the games allowed for the crane to not grip quite as tightly until a certain threshold of money was reached; a player would almost require that fortune of arriving after that point to have a fair chance to use their skill, at which time the counter would reset.

As there were some families here with a wide range of ages among their children, Kicks hoped some of them had tried and failed, and that the machine hadn't payed out in a few days. That would improve his chances.

He put in his two dollars—quite steep for a crane game, but he was just killing time—and aimed the claw over his prize. From where he stood, he was lined up pretty well with the small box on the left-and-right axis. He moved his head around the side of the machine and looked through that glass panel as well, ensuring he was all set in the forward-backward axis, keeping an eye on his thirty-second timer.

With twelve seconds left, he nudged the joystick forward the tiniest bit, and then back again, causing the loose claw to swing in the air. He pressed the button on the panel to drop the crane.

As he'd hoped, the claw continued to swing on its way down, and one of the three fingers therefore caught underneath the small box. The claw closed, and the other two joined it, meeting underneath the watch.

That wasn't itself a guarantee, though. There was no way to tell how much the fingers moved independently in the air, and the box could still fall out if it moved at all within the wide enclosure once off the ground.

The claw settled for a moment before rising. As Kicks feared, the small box shifted its weight, no longer supported by the small rocks that made up the floor of the game. By some miracle, it didn't fall off right away—the watch remained within his grasp.

But he still remained cautiously optimistic. The moment of truth would arrive when the crane reached the height of the glass box, returning to the arm. The jolt of that sudden stop would certainly cause the claw to swing again, and if he was not the lucky designated winner, the fingers would not hold tight enough for the box to survive the shock.

"Hey yo, Kicks! What're you—" a familiar voice called from his left. He turned his head to greet his friends. "Oh, you are shitting me! Guys, check Kicks out!"

Kicks turned his head, but by the sounds of his friends' extended 'oohs' and 'wows' it was too late. He'd missed it.

The claw had reached its home over the chute down to the prize door, open and empty.

He slouched his shoulders some in defeat.

"Kicks, how did you do that, man?" shouted one of the guys as the group approached.

"Yeah man, that was nuts! I've never seen someone beat one of these things before!" applauded another.

"What are you...?" Kicks began to ask. His eyes widened. Had he missed it?

He eagerly crouched down and pushed back the small door at the bottom of the machine. He reached his hand inside and felt around the dark black floor.

His fingers brushed against something. A small box. He gripped it gently, and pulled his arm out as he rose to his feet.

He'd done it.

He didn't miss the box falling back *into* the machine, but out of it! His friends had distracted him, but they showed up just in time to watch him successfully carry the smartwatch all the way across the inside of the game and drop it unceremoniously—but triumphantly—into his hands.

Kicks had trouble paying attention the rest of the day. It wasn't that he was distracted; he did play along, and he did enjoy himself. The Del Toro boys bowled a few games, laughing and riffing on each other all the way. They paused for some concession food in the late afternoon, then walked down the street and back to one of the older guy's apartment. But all through it, Kicks couldn't get his mind off of that amazing win. He held the smartwatch close to his chest the whole way, and what information he retained of every bowl and every joke was prefaced with the prize in his hands. The odds weren't astronomical by any means, but things like this didn't happen to people like him.

Was this God, somehow telling him that he was looked after—that he was loved—in His strange and mysterious way?

He couldn't say for certain. But he found these thoughts filling his lonely walk home. The others begged him not to go just yet, but Kicks worried for his grandmother, and looked forward to making dinner with her on Sundays.

Though it was still summertime by calendar, the shift into fall had already begun—the sun had begun setting earlier in the past few weeks. Not by much, but enough that it was a dim blue beneath the long shadows cast by the low buildings, and the sky was filled not only with burnt oranges and golds, but also pinks and silvers. These were colors you simply couldn't find anywhere else. They were a big part of why Kicks loved the desert.

75

He could see clearly enough in front of him, but there was just enough darkness far and around him that he didn't realize that the strange, flopping shape at the edge of the light was bounding towards him until it was already too close for him to flee.

He turned to run anyway, putting his Adidas Duramo 9s to good use.

His affordable shoes were not effective enough, though. The figure behind him was fast, despite the apparent incoherence displayed by its silhouette. It leapt at and lunged for him. As he heard the final pound of its bony foot against the concrete, he turned his head. The creature pounced on him, and he turned in mid-air as it pinned him to the ground.

Kicks looked up into the snarling face of his attacker. The blue hue beneath the shade obscured it some, and the muted sky did little to aid him, but from mere inches away, he could see the skin of the man looming over him was greyed and battered. His cheeks were receded. Deflated. His chin and nose had decayed so much that what flesh remained around the holes had tightened and adapted to its new form. The revealed bones were stained brown under chips of dried blood. And his eyes... they were less than lifeless. They were devoid and vacant—no light reflected from them, but just as much, no darkness seeped out. They were pure, perfect, and impossibly black.

Kicks couldn't help but look down, as if to survey his pinned body and document what the horror did to him. As his eyes struggled to peer through the darkness—a task made even more difficult by the man hunched hungrily over him—he couldn't help but notice them. His attacker's shoes.

They were easier to see even in the low light thanks to their garish yellow shade. There was no doubt in Kicks' mind; they were the same Nike Air Max 97s he had seen only hours ago.

76

He looked up, only now recognizing the face of the horrific creature.

The undead man hissed a low grumble, his spindly hands patting at his prey's torso. His horrid fingers travelled down to Kicks' waist, and as he felt the coarse skin grind against the denim of his jeans, Kicks sucked in air, knowing what he was after.

He pulled out the smartwatch box, eyeing it carefully as he held it to his face. The creature looked down at him again, before bounding away down the street; neither back the direction he came from, nor resuming the path he had been travelling.

Kicks sat up, collecting himself. He patted his leg as if to ensure he had comprehended what just happened. The box was truly gone. He had been waiting to open it and set it up until he got home, to ensure it could be charged. Now it was gone.

Kicks stood up and shook his head. He was breathing heavily, his mind catching up with the shock as he realized what he'd just experienced.

He could have died! He was almost killed by that creature. If he thought he was lucky before, he had to believe someone was watching out for him now. That man—that zombie—was fast, and strong. No doubt it could have killed him. But it didn't. He survived. He was allowed to survive.

He pressed his fingers to his lips and looked up at the dimming Las Vegas sky. Kicks silently thanked whoever might be out there that someone was pulling the strings, and that they apparently had his back.

Issue 9
Intermission

Lady Harrow expected the next few days to be wild with business opportunities and petty skirmishes alike coming to meet the near-indisputable supremacy of the Del Toro gang. With the Sons of Washington out of the way, there were no more major groups limiting their territory in Las Vegas.

They still had some challengers, of course. Most dealers didn't have a territory, per se, but did work in specific areas to reach their regulars more easily. There would certainly be at least half a dozen labs in the city that would need to be decommissioned so as not to poison the Del Toros' false supply. And the former crime syndicates had other families that would try to reclaim the business of their imprisoned associates—the most notable in this regard were the Italians. But the Menteur's associates were only too happy to handle these nuisances in the name of cooperation and success.

However, much to her surprise, there was little talk at all from the Mexican organization.

Sunday passed with silence. That wasn't terribly unusual; most of the Del Toros were relatively devoted to their faith. Harrow didn't go looking for them, and she knew they wouldn't come looking for her yet, either.

But Monday... There should have been a noticeable change in the air on Monday. Even though her regularly scheduled appointments with the Del Toros weren't until Wednesday, with no one else to limit their scope, she was shocked no one had approached her about next steps for both of their agencies.

Tuesday, too, saw no changes in the structure of the city underbelly. There was no major paradigm shift. No evidence that product was still moving in the areas where she and Legacy had halted the market. For some reason, the Del Toros weren't filing into the vacancies. In fact, it almost seemed like demand had vanished in their own parts of Las Vegas. But Harrow didn't want to get too involved in their practices; they couldn't know she was manipulating them from the outside. The Menteur had to remain just a supplier, not a leader.

So when Wednesday came, she proceeded as she always had. Hopefully, Jenna would be willing and empowered to purchase significantly more imaginary orders, or else inform her supplier of new opportunities within the organization, and across the city. Although she wanted nothing more than to seek out more information on their new immediate goal, dropping out of the long game altogether wasn't an option either. It was vital that appearances be kept up.

Harrow opted, therefore, to leave Legacy behind for this encounter. It should appear as though nothing had changed for the Menteur, and that meant no new representatives. She parted ways with her lover after resealing their home behind the illusory brick wall, taking her own car to the Laundromat she frequented each week.

Stepping into the building, something immediately came off to her as not right. She didn't catch exactly how immediately, but it wasn't long before she learned this dread was not misplaced.

79

She looked over to the counter area as she always did, to signal her client of her arrival. But Jenna wasn't there.

It was some nerdy freckled man she'd never seen before. She instinctively checked her watch to ensure the day was correct. It was. Jenna should have been there. Hell, it shouldn't matter what day it was, she was a manager.

She walked over to the counter and waited for the attention of the teenaged human. She wasn't one to use her form for favors—it was disgusting to her, to be lusted for by, and attractive to, humans; particularly ignorant underdeveloped ones—but evidently it wasn't something one needed to make an effort to do to get use out of. The man-child came to help her nearly right away.

"Yes, ma'am, how can I help you?" he asked with a skip in his voice.

"Is Jenna here today?" Harrow countered with her own direct question. She felt no need for additional details or cover stories today, and certainly not with him.

"Oh, uh, sorry. She was actually let go." he replied, eyes shifting in apology.

"What? When? And why?" This was unacceptable. What had Heraldo done?

"I— I don't know why." the boy was able to stammer out. "It was Monday; after her shift the owner came in and fired her. I didn't hear the conversation, it was in the office. But she stormed out; she's not allowed on property for a year."

Lady Harrow turned away. She didn't need to hear any more, and it was unlikely she'd find any other useful information here anyway. She walked outside in concerned thought. Who was she supposed to contact now? Who was doing the purchasing and dealing for this area?

When she walked through the sliding doors and back outside, she realized where she'd gotten her initial sense of alarm. Kicks wasn't here. None of the Del Toros were loitering outside.

"Shit. What's going on?" Harrow spat in confusion and dismay. She reached for her phone and searched her contacts for Legacy. After two tones, she answered. "Jieadea? There's a problem here. Where are you?"

"I'm at the Canals. What's wrong?" the voice on the other end replied with concern.

"Meet me at the Del Toro's cell phone store. Something's wrong with the Laundromat, we might—" Harrow cut herself off. "I don't know what to do. Just come meet me?"

"Uh, yeah. Sure, on my way. See you soon, R'Bec."

"See you soon." She tapped her phone to hang up the call. Her hands were shaking. She almost thought to reach for her globe, but this was not one of her nightmares.

Lady Harrow walked back to her car, careful not to draw attention to herself. There were several options for what was going on here, and any of them could mean she was in danger.

First, and most preferable, was that Jenna had just been caught by the Laundromat owners for her drug trafficking and fired. Given the police apparently didn't carry her out, she wasn't arrested. This seemed unlikely, as her shipments were cleverly concealed as laundry supplies, and were mostly fake or incorporeal.

Second, one of the former crime organizations, or someone related to them, had launched a counterattack on the Del Toros, having figured out that she was working on the Mexican gang's behalf, even if they didn't know it. This would imply the whole drug ring was compromised, and their opponents wouldn't be as kind as she had been to them. It didn't perfectly explain why Jenna had been fired as opposed to not showing up, but who knew how the vengeful criminals might have tried to coax the Mexicans out of their hiding places?

A third option was that idiot cop who had staked out the Sons of Washington. There was no way they were able to plan and execute a stakeout on that golf store, much less on the same night Harrow and Legacy planned to take them out. It was too convenient and too effective for Las Vegas police. So then they must have been tailing her, which could mean they figured out who her contacts were. This was the least likely scenario, as Jenna was fired, not arrested. But it could be that the cops somehow detained the Del Toro leadership, and with them out of the picture, the owners of the Laundromat felt empowered to act on suspicions they already had.

Regardless of which of these possibilities was correct, this presented a problem for Lady Harrow's plan. Without a puppet organization to act as the sole distributor of her false product for the city, the remnants of her previous targets would simply reform and resume their positions with actual narcotics. She had to figure out exactly what happened and work with Legacy to create a new strategy.

She reached her car and sat down in the driver's seat. She was only inside for a few minutes, but the heat was unbearable in the black sedan. Fortunately, the air conditioner was already at its lowest setting, and at full blast, so it wouldn't be too hot for too long.

As she started her car, she heard an unfamiliar click from behind her. Concerned with the sign of apparent disrepair in her otherwise new-enough sedan, she turned around—only for her forehead to meet with the end of a pistol.

In the seat behind her sat a young woman, her gun pressed against Harrow's face.

"Alright, H, let's have a chat." Jenna said.

Harrow reached for her keys to turn off the ignition. Jenna nudged the barrel against her illusory skin.

"Keep it on; it's too damn hot to talk without AC." Her eyes were cold and determined. Something was off, and she clearly thought Harrow was involved.

"Jenna, I don't know what's going on. They told me you were fired, I'm trying to figure out—"

The woman in her rear seat once again nudged the end of her weapon, prompting Harrow to stop. Jenna lifted it slightly from her forehead, before setting it down beside her.

"I know you don't know, dummy." Jenna said through a coy smile. "I'm asking for your help, not getting revenge."

"What? Help with what?" Harrow said quickly, a look of confusion plainly painted on her face. She stopped to compose herself, clearing her mind to ask the right questions. "What exactly happened?"

Jenna looked out the window at the Laundromat's entrance. "New management."

"Someone else owns the Laundromat?"

"No. Someone else owns the Del Toros." Jenna replied firmly. From the sound of her voice, her stomach was in an uproar with anger. "I know, I know; I'm being melodramatic. Let me try to get it straight.

"So you've heard of Marco Nieve, right?"

"Vaguely. I recognize the name."

"He runs Snow Dynamics Enterprises, down in New Jackson. He's also that superhero, Shatterbug."

"So he runs the Del Toros now?" Harrow asked with confusion. What would a self-proclaimed hero want with a drug ring? Especially in another state?

"No, and shush." Jenna replied with only slight annoyance. "The first thing he fought, that crazy big monster that was plastered all over the internet? That thing was a person, and its name was Julio. He was a Del Toro lieutenant down in the NJSU territory. Apparently, he's gone a bit soft on crime since then."

"He's still aware? He's not just some hulking monster?"

"He is, but he's also a monster. He came up here, smashed up the headquarters, killed all the leadership and put himself in charge. He's just so big, like some invincible punching bag, no one tried to stop him. But he's using the Del Toros to try to bring down all the drug cartels in Vegas, including our own. He dismissed the lieutenants and killed anyone who disagreed. No point in having dealers without coke, so he arranged for us to get taken out of our covers.

"Whoever's left of the Del Toros works for him now, killing criminals and burning product. And..." she trailed off, hesitating. "He's got his eyes set on the Menteur, and on you, H."

Harrow was shocked. All of her hard work seemed to have been for nothing. Her plan was ruined. And this Julio's plan was flawed, it wasn't going to solve anything. As long as the underworld of Las Vegas didn't at least believe they had access to drugs, there would always be a drug trade. That was just how economy worked.

"How do you know all this?" she asked the woman sitting behind her.

"Kicks." she answered plainly. "He's still with the Del Toros—he's gotta provide for his grandma, and protect her—but after I got dropped, he found me and filled me in. He's scared, H. You gotta help me take this guy down."

There was no need for hesitation. Even if for some reason she didn't want to help Jenna and Kicks, she still had a duty to Las Vegas, and to her own mission, to restore the Del Toros. "Of course, J. You don't even need to ask. But first, we gotta meet up with my partner."

"The Mentuer?" Jenna asked, puzzled.

"No, new girl. She's called Legacy."

"You people and your nicknames. Alright, that's fine. Let's go."

The two women drove for a few minutes to the small device store which formerly housed the Del Toros' secondary storage and dealers. As Legacy would be a while longer coming from the Strip, they opted to wait in the car. There was little reason to go inside anyway; Jenna informed Harrow that she had met up with her associates stationed here to find the same result: Julio was able to get their positions revoked, and they had been ejected from the organization.

When Legacy arrived, having flagged down a lift from a somewhat dazed young man, she joined the two in the car. After introductions, Jenna imparted the rest of her knowledge.

"Julio is still operating out of the old headquarters. It's much less guarded now, but still basically a fortress. No doubt he'll have bounties on both our heads."

"But those kids are your friends. They're just enforcers, it's not like they're devoted to his ideology. It's not a cult." Legacy said. She was visibly perturbed by this inconvenience in their plot.

"You're right, but like you said, they *are* just kids. They're scared, and he's given them a very good reason to be. They might hesitate, but if he's there, I think they'll follow him in the end."

"So we need to be stealthy. This isn't a meeting, it's a break-in." Lady Harrow proclaimed.

"Right. More than that, it's an assassination."

"You wanna kill this guy?" Legacy asked with a raised eyebrow.

"I think—if we even can—that it's the only way we can set things right. We're not gonna be able to just wear him down and convince him to leave. He's enormous and powerful, and we're not superheroes."

Jenna's last statement resonated with Harrow, and put her in unease. She couldn't place why, but it didn't matter. The feeling dissipated as quickly as it had appeared, thanks to an empathetic look from Legacy.

"Okay then," Legacy started. "Let's go to these 'headquarters' and them 'im out."

"Tonight." Jenna declared. "We don't know what Julio has at his disposal, or how aggressive he'll be. We attack during the day and we'll get way more attention than we need, giving him a chance to escape. We'll stake the place out for now, and make our strategy—both for getting in, and for what to do when we're done."

"Right." Harrow agreed.

The trio didn't see Julio at all during their stakeout. If Kicks was to be believed, it was unlikely he would want to be seen in broad daylight. However, this gave the women the opportunity to eye the compound carefully in preparation for their intrusion.

The Del Toro headquarters in Las Vegas was nestled inside a seemingly ordinary building near one of the lesser casinos. It was an old and decrepit structure, but it had the advantage of being large and multi-functional—several of the nearby businesses made use of it. This made it an ideal hiding spot for the center of an organized street gang. With so many people coming and going for so many different reasons, it would be easy to be swept up in the crowd. But, indeed, most of the interior was used by the infamous—and now only—drug cartel.

During the day, various enforcers could be seen mulling about, but it was difficult to gauge exactly how many were inside. As the sun started to set, the night shift security guards started to arrive. With them, and among them, were the Del Toros that would be stationed there overnight as well. And as new faces started to leave and familiar ones left with no return, a plan began to form.

"There should only be about six or seven now, give or take depending on how many security guards they've got roped in." Legacy noted.

"I know for a fact only one of those white guys is not ours—or theirs, I guess." Jenna caught herself. She clearly wasn't willing accept her fate with the Del Toros yet.

"There's no open windows." Lady Harrow said as she opened the car door, returning from her scouting mission around the building. She slammed it shut just loudly enough to sound realistically purposeful without standing out. "And what few windows there *are* look into independent units. That leaves three doors into the main complex, where Julio will be."

"If the night shift is anything like the day, another patrol should come around in just a minute." Legacy began, adding her own observations gathered from her fixed position. "We know two of the three guards are compromised, so—"

"We'll have to watch their whole cycle once to see when the odd man out shows up in the order." Jenna interrupted. From the look on Legacy's face, she stole the words right from her mouth. "He'll be less attentive, giving us a better opportunity to get inside with a little more noise."

"Which door do we breach?" Legacy asked with a tone just teetering on the edge of mocking.

"The side door." Harrow answered promptly. "It's flanked on both sides by independent units, so there's probably just a long hallway from there into the rest of the building. Less space to be seen in or heard from."

"Right, good point." Jenna applauded. "Now there's just the question of how to fight Julio…"

"Just take the shots you can, and leave the rest to me." Harrow replied with an encouraging look from Legacy.

"You been holding some skills out on me, H?"

"You never asked." she said flatly, betrayed only slightly by the hint of a smile.

The three women sat in the car, waiting for the security team's cycle to shuffle through. One of the Del Toro men was the first to come out. About half-an-hour later, right on cue, was their ignorant target.

"Now, we go now!" Legacy said as she started to reach for her door handle.

"Shush!" Jenna shouted through gritted teeth. "Not yet!"

They waited briefly for the man to pass, ensuring he didn't hear anything.

"We have to wait until after the first guy goes back in." Harrow said gently. "That'll give us the greatest amount of time without interruption. We'll have thirty minutes, plus this guy's whole patrol. Not that we should need it, but it's forward thinking."

Legacy grumbled with the logic of their plan. She clearly wasn't used to democratic strategizing.

The car was silent while the guard circled the building just as the first did, performing his routine checks of each door and window as he went. Only when he re-entered the building's security office did anyone feel the opportunity to breathe deeply again. They sat waiting, chatting and joking—always with one pair of eyes on the warm night outside and the quiet, looming structure their target resided in—until thirty minutes later, the third member of the security team emerged. This one, like the first, was a Del Toro operative, working to protect her comrades inside. As such, she was more thorough than the man before, but worked more quickly and efficiently on her patrol.

Again, only when she completed her rounds did the trio let out a breath of relief, returning to their vigilant conversations. They took note as the first guard began his second walkabout of the night, marking the restarting of the cycle. Although as before, the three women were silent in breath and unblinking in gaze, they each had a hand on their respective door handles, eager to breach the shared facility and reclaim the street gang from the murderous thug.

After what seemed like hours or even days, the Del Toro enforcer returned to his post a few minutes later, marking the end of his patrol.

Lady Harrow, Legacy, and Jenna all sprang into action with urgency unrivaled. They leapt from the car like cats and made way for the side of the wide building. Harrow did not even bother with locking the vehicle, at the risk of someone noticing any lights that may flicker or fade. They walked briskly, but with care, toward the intended entry point.

Taking the lead, Harrow turned the door handle and peeked inside.

Behind it, as expected, was a hallway. It wasn't terribly long, maybe forty feet at most. It was difficult to judge in the dark. A few doors lined either side with no clear uniformity in spacing. The larger expanse at the end of the corridor was lit, though dimly, but no one was nearby or looking in their direction. Harrow hurried in, bidding her companions to follow closely.

She quickly summoned her preferred weapon at her side: a pistol resembling a flintlock piece in design, with a pointlessly large barrel and hammer. Were a specialist to actually look at it, the gun wouldn't be able to fire a pea, much less a bullet. But it was a figment of her imagination, as were its rounds and their velocities, laws of physics be damned.

A sound behind her told Harrow that Jenna had noticed, and that she nearly tripped over herself in surprise and confusion. She glanced back in time to see Legacy shushing her with her finger, her face trying to assure the human woman that they would explain later. Harrow turned her attention back to their sly progression, but signaled to Jenna with her free hand to ready her own weapon.

She then conjured an illusion of a long knife—nearly great enough to be called a short sword—for Legacy to wield. She tied its permanence into her mind, drawing on all of the synapses in her brain so she wouldn't have to actively think about it to keep it in play. Harrow would have preferred to give her lover a firearm as well, but as she didn't know how guns actually worked, it would be nearly impossible for her to be aware enough of when Legacy fired to create those associated rounds as well as her own.

As they reached the end of the hall, most of the greater room ahead came into view. There were five Del Toro enforcers in this area, with no sign of Julio. They brushed his absence off as him being in one of the adjoining rooms, and began to strategize with each other with gestures in the dim light.

Three of the men were sitting around a small card table. Two appeared to be playing some sort of game, though it couldn't be discerned from the women's vantage. The other was watching them, talking and laughing along with them as they discussed the game and other tangential subjects. A fourth gangster was sitting on her phone nearby, blissfully unaware of the conversation her associates were enveloped in.

The fifth was quite a young man—practically a boy, really. Too young to be in a street gang, and yet forced to by circumstance and pressure. Harrow recognized him immediately; his stoic face was the only one trying to do a good job, trying to keep a lookout on the empty room and be a good little soldier. She gulped at the sight of the human she couldn't help but pity. She cursed the forces of chance.

Why did Kicks have to be here?

Harrow glanced back to see if Jenna had noticed, too. By the look on her silent face, she had. But Legacy quietly reminded them with a stern expression that it couldn't be helped. They didn't have to hurt him. The weapons were for Julio; Lady Harrow could dispatch these enforcers with non-lethal force.

She stood up proudly and strode into the room, allowing herself to be cast in the somewhat brighter light of the expansive arena in the main portion of the structure. As she did so, she created another illusion to mirror her already-present weapon in the other hand, and took aim for Kicks. Unfortunately, as he was the only one paying attention, he had to be the first to go down.

She fired.

It wasn't a proper explosion within the chamber, of course. As she pulled the illusory trigger, she willed the hammer to move as one might expect, forced fire and smoke to pop where it would collide with the gunpowder that wasn't really there, and then summoned a shell at the very end of the gun. It had a trajectory that would land precisely where she imagined it would, but that was in fact impossible for how she was aiming the gun, if perhaps only by a few degrees. No one would notice, though, if a bullet aimed around the area of one's shoulder from twenty feet away might hit one's heart instead.

And so it did. The overly-large round slugged into Kicks' chest with real force, prompting Harrow to replace it with an imaginary hole and plenty of fake blood while her target fell to the ground. Though it took only a fraction more than a second or two, it was forever to Harrow's eyes before the childlike human hit the ground and fell into unconsciousness.

The other four Del Toros collected themselves at the intrusion. They were not adept in quickly combating a surprise attack, so two more were eliminated before the others got an opportunity to take a shot.

Although they wouldn't be able to tell, Lady Harrow was creating tiny illusions of an impertinent material to deflect their incoming fire. It took a tremendous amount of focus, and in doing so, she was unable to create illusions of her own rounds with any reasonable accuracy, but she continued to let the hammer of her gun explode again and again to appear as though she was unrelenting in her attacks.

Finally, her opponents' magazines were spent, and she let off a single shot for each, wishing for her false rounds to reach them squarely in the forehead. They would wake up with awful bruises, but for now, they needed to believe they would never wake up at all, so a hole and blood was all they saw on each others' faces. Their brains fooled themselves with their imagined demise, forcing their knees to give before they passed out in shock.

The dust of the one-sided battle settled as Harrow's illusions dissolved into a black smoke before fading into the air. All three intruders now fully entered the otherwise empty room, save for the half-dozen support pillars and the now-overturned card table.

Lady Harrow and Jenna rushed over to kneel beside Kicks, ensuring he was unharmed. The fake blood was gone now, and she moved his shirt aside to ensure she had timed the dissolution of her bullet correctly, preventing an actual wound.

Just a bruise. He would be fine.

"Since when can you—" Jenna began to say, before being cut off.

An unexpected and inexplicable noise grumbled from behind Harrow. Beside the hallway, the room they stood in now dipped further back somewhat, rather than being a separate room joined by a doorway. It was darker there, the dim lights in the middle of the arena having difficulty to illuminate the concealed niche. Still, she could make out the clear silhouette of a huge, muscled brute of a man struggling to fit comfortably upon a shaky and over-encumbered throne.

The figure rose with a huff, somewhere between a snarl and a stifle, its full shape and size coming into view for the three women.

He was twice Lady Harrow's size, impressively just short enough to fit inside the tall room without crouching, though he was hunched by the sheer weight of his ludicrous arms and legs, which she estimated were also about twice as thick as her torso. His chest was bare and scarred; what were at first glance tattoos were in fact actual tears in his greyed flesh, peeking into a void-like darkness which almost seemed to writhe under his skin, giving his muscles a life all their own. His eyes looked down at them with the same unreflective blackness, a perfect shadow without gloss or sheen that could rival the expanse of space in its ability to terrify. He loomed over them with fingers half the length of her forearm curled and balled into fists. He shook his head idly—but for a skull so large as he had, it was a violent movement anyway—to brush aside the unkempt and matted hair that had fallen in front of his face. He breathed deeply, clearly unimpressed by the Telignen's performance.

"Julio Carillo!" Jenna shouted with only a tiny catch in her voice. Even this was an impressive feat—Harrow was without words, herself.

"*¿Cómo?* Where did you learn that name, girl?" His voice was deep and harsh. It was as though every twist of his vocal cords was tense—not out of anger, but out of pain. The sounds seem to come from his whole body, not just his throat. It didn't echo or reverberate at all; it was a constant and continuous coarseness that had each of the women cringing with each syllable, as though hearing it hurt him to speak also hurt them. "Oh, I see. You're one of the dealers I got fired. Good, good. Now I won't need to have these *idiotas* hunt you down.

"Anyway, Julio is dead."

The behemoth lifted his left fist up with impossible speed, slamming it down on the concrete floor just short of where Jenna and Harrow were standing, on either side of the unconscious Kicks. His hulking fingers cratered the ground beneath them, and without even needing to look, a crack told Harrow they had crushed something else, too.

She wasn't sure if she would have the courage to check for the source of the noise, for fear her instincts were correct, but her body took control. Her neck turned and angled her head down to see—as the creature's hand rose and returned to his side—that it had broken Kicks' legs.

They were mangled and bleeding. Harrow thought she would never be able to look away as tears welled in her eyes, but Jenna's words brought her back to the present, and her face returned to the visage of their target above them.

"You're a monster! You horrible piece of—"

"Yeah, I'm a monster. Didn't you hear?" He smiled, revealing his yellowed teeth. Each individual piece of tiny calcium was flanked by darkness. Behind that wicked smile seemed to stretch pure emptiness inside his throat, with nothing else visible despite the hole in his face being as wide as Harrow's hand. "I'm Titan Black."

Issue 10
Priest of Pain

Harrow's mind worked at dizzying speeds. As the great fist of the man once called Julio came crashing down once again, threatening to bury her and Jenna in the rubble among Kicks' still limp and unconscious body, she took aim with her imaginary gun and fired.

The fake bullet came whizzing out the end of the chamber, rushing at Harrow's side. She didn't even look where she was aiming; there wasn't time. It flew straight for Jenna, sending her flying back. It was a larger and more forceful round than she typically used, and she didn't replace it with a hole or blood when it vanished. It existed solely to push her associate out of the way of the oncoming attack.

She too was thrown back by the force of Titan Black descending on the ground where she had stood half a second ago. Her instincts kicked in for more than just Jenna's good, allowing her to try and leap out of the way just enough to avoid the blow without injury, though the sheer mass of the behemoth's body slamming into the concrete put her off balance in the air, and she landed shaky before tipping over.

There was no time to waste. The man now called Titan was rushing her, unwilling to give her even a moment to collect herself or return to her feet. Harrow could only futilely try to roll to the side, partly in escape and partly in an attempt to shield herself from the approaching shock.

But it didn't come.

She rolled back to her vulnerable position to see what had happened. Black's fist was upon her, being held above her body. Between it and her was a short but menacing blade, outstretched and struggling against the might of the huge thing that was once a man.

Legacy was shaking in her efforts to hold her small sword as long as she could, her grunts becoming more pitiful after a few seconds. Despite the sharp edge pressing against the monster's skin, he would not yield. In fact, it almost seemed like it was breaking through the greyed flesh, but that some shadowy substance inside of him was holding it back. In any case, Harrow put her at ease by rolling fully out of the way of the attack, allowing her partner to release the beast's fist.

Of course, Titan Black was no fool. He did not let that arm fall to the ground—that would be a pointless waste of energy—nor did he allow Lady Harrow to be free without a fight. His other hand came at her like an enormous paddle in an attempt to knock her over, while the first steadied himself and acted as a barrier between her and Legacy.

She took aim with her gun, hoping it would prove a more effective defense than the sword she had tied inside her mind. Again, she fired off a round meant to generate force more than to pierce, although she would attempt to push it through his hand, if she could.

The power she put behind her illusion was enough to halt Black's swing, and even stagger his footing. But as it tried to penetrate the torn skin, even as she willed the bullet-shaped collection of dust and mental trickery to stay together and press forward...

His skin was broken. But the *thing* on the other side—the blackness that dwelled within him and seemed to protect and empower him—resisted in a way Harrow had never witnessed or imagined before. It refused to budge one way or the other to the might of her mind, and more than that, it was fighting against the fabric of the imaginary round. The tiniest teeth poked out from Titan's veins, clawing and spearing at the oversized casing, forcing it to dissolve even as the Telignen bound it to realty in her mind, too.

All at once, the bullet shattered into a cloud of dust, letting Harrow see inside her opponent's palm. It was empty. Devoid of life and light. Yet still, something inside was somehow alive; it squirmed and twisted beneath his flesh like some huge parasite.

And that was when she started to consider what she was up against. But she needed more information before committing to a conclusion.

"How are you doing that?" she shouted up in terror at the villain, who had regained his balance, but was temporarily mesmerized by his own display of power.

"I'm not doing anything, *chica*." he declared with more depth and pain than perhaps he even realized. "You can't control your own blood, and neither can I."

Legacy took this opportunity to ready her own attack. She leapt into the air to stab her large knife as high as she could: into Black's shoulder blade.

Again, it broke flesh, but the black 'blood' inside refused to grant it any further passage, trying instead to destroy the invading illusion.

Jenna was now able to get to her feet, regaining the wind knocked out of her by Harrow's violent defense of her. She took aim with her own real weapon and fired on Titan Black's head.

As one of her shots hit the side of his face, inches away from his unreflective eye, he covered himself with his gargantuan forearm in surprise. Three more bullets made their way for the meat shield.

Each of the physical rounds shot through the bulging skin, which appeared to be marred and scratched from similar past experiences, with each scar showing only more of the perfect darkness beneath the surface. Once these new bullets reached that barrier, they shattered into insignificant shrapnel, some pieces becoming embedded in the grey flesh surrounding the wound, with the rest falling to the floor pointlessly.

This interruption did nothing to stop the shadow's work on Legacy's blade. The tiny tentacle-like spines erupting from his back lunged at the false metal decisively, dissolving the illusion and the threads that bound it inside Harrow's mind.

The strain was agonizing, like a sudden and sharp migraine in the back edges of her brain. Lady Harrow gripped her temples in pain, before the sword became dust and the dust became nothing, leaving her winded and shaken, but otherwise unharmed. She had never experienced this before. Her illusions dissipated constantly, and she had broken binds in her mind before; she did so nearly every day. Why was this different? How was it even possible?

"R'Bec, you thinking what I'm thinking?" Legacy shouted from around Titan Black. He tried to turn around and swing another great fist at the Svuarti. He was impossibly fast for his size, but the change of direction gave her more time to dodge than if he had already been facing her.

Harrow pushed her concerns about the pain she had just gone through to the back of her mind, returning to her initial conclusions. She was indeed thinking exactly what Legacy was.

"Jenna, stay back. This thing's more dangerous than it looks." Harrow begged of her associate.

"It looks really flippin' dangerous, H!" she shouted. "He's a freak! How do we kill him with this firepower?"

"We can't. He's already dead." Legacy informed her coldly as she jumped and slid around Black's arms, trying to break his defense and get back to her partners.

"He's the source of the zombies. I'm sure of it." Harrow said solemnly. It made sense, all the signs pointed to it. He had the same rotting skin and the same empty eyes she had seen that night by her home, and as what was described to her by the countless others who had seen the creatures terrorizing the Las Vegas underworld. He was bigger than them, of course, but that wouldn't be surprising for their progenitor; if anything, it was only more evidence. All that was missing was the how, and the why.

She couldn't think too much on it now, though. At this announcement, Black's eyebrow cocked with interest, and his attention turned to the Telignen.

She countered with a huge metal shield between her and Titan, arching up and around her. His fist met the barrier, which strained against his massive form. He pressed against it with more and more effort, though without apparent strain on his part. In only a few seconds, the illusion was broken, and he smashed through to crater the concrete it protected.

A few seconds was all Lady Harrow needed to get out of the way though, stepping back just a few feet to avoid the blow.

"The source of the *what?*" Jenna yelled quizzically. With this, Black shifted his focus to her, putting his mauled forearm in front of him and running towards her with speed that can only be achieved with terrifying strength. He intended to completely bulldoze her.

It took Harrow a moment to imagine, but with ten feet separating the two, she had time to conjure a five-foot wrecking ball swinging from the ceiling, right in Titan's path.

He wasn't able to stop in time, blind rage keeping his legs rushing towards Jenna. The sphere hit him squarely in the side of his huge abdomen, just below his ribcage. The illusion dissolved immediately, but it had enough power behind it to knock him aside some distance, scraping his feet against the floor and leaving a wake of broken rock.

However, as he got up, it was quite apparent that he was completely unfazed by even that. He looked down at his side to see an apparent bruise; the grey skin where the ball had impacted was slightly darker, but not broken. He grinned.

Black laughed. "I see you, *amiga*. Trying to look for monsters in the dark; you think you're a hero, like me."

His smile turned into a sneer, and his brow furrowed in rage. "Well we're not heroes!"

At this declaration, he moved with more speed than he'd shown in their battle so far, leaping forward from the ground and flying through the air, directly toward Lady Harrow.

She tried again to raise an illusion to defend herself in the same way as before, but Black let his clenched fists fall on either side of her display, meeting behind her to trap her in his arms. Once he stopped, he headbutted the shield, forcing it to completely shatter back into its base particles, and leaving a slightly smaller bruise on his forehead.

He nearly screamed at Harrow, his engorged face right in front of her. She felt his voice in her bones—both the hatred, and the agony. "*Heroes* try to be *better!*" He lifted one arm up and used the other to brush her aside with tremendous force, causing her to slide into one of the pillars, all before she could even register his words. She coughed as her back collided with the stone column.

"*Heroes* don't do the wrong things, even for the right reasons!" Titan bellowed, bringing both his fists down on either side of where he stood. He was using more energy now, fueled by an inexplicable rage, and so the sheer power of his move knocked Jenna and Legacy off balance.

From the ground, Jenna tried to get in another few shots, hoping the distraction would give someone—anyone—a chance to gain an upper hand against the invincible horror. His decayed skin became a small black circle in each spot she hit, but he didn't even pretend to flinch as the shadow inside of him filled in the space. As more of Julio broke away, more of Titan Black rose to the surface. It was more than just his skin being torn apart; it almost seemed to Harrow that with every wound, with every square inch that his blood repaired, more of the man was lost to the monster.

He snapped his huge fingers, creating a disturbance in the air's pressure that caused all three women to reach for their eardrums. Jenna dropped her gun, the pieces inside becoming useless with the deafening crack, which subsided as quickly as it had rung.

Titan marched towards Harrow gravely, his mighty arms swinging at his side and his head held high, looking down at his opponent. "*I'm* a killer. *You're* a drug lord; or lady, whatever. We're *not* heroes."

He started to press his hand against her, applying pressure evenly throughout her body, pushing her against the pillar she leaned against. He was trying to crush her.

But her body wasn't human, as much as it looked the part. She could still talk.

"Yes, we are." she strained, the pain in her bones not yet unbearable.

"No, we're *not.*"

"Yes," she started again. His incessant stress on her chest was starting to weigh down on her speech. "Yes you *are*, Julio."

His hesitation was obvious. He stopped adding more pressure, though Harrow still couldn't move.

"Inciting positive change is heroic." she continued through heavy breath. "Trying to make the world safer is heroic. Not asking for reward or recognition *is* heroic."

Titan Black started to release her, although slowly, still skeptical. As his face came back into view for her, she saw he was looking at her with interest, curious in what she had to say. She was getting through to him.

"Shatterbug is a hero, yes, but he's not the only kind of hero. Not all heroes wear capes, or suits, or are known by name. Not all heroes are always right, or always sure of themselves." Lady Harrow knew how to appeal to him. Jenna said he was Shatterbug's first opponent. He obviously had a complicated relationship with his own morality. All he needed was validation. "You took down the leaders of a major drug operation. Even though you killed them, and are using the rest of the Del Toros to kill anyone involved with drug trafficking, you have a noble goal. You're a hero, Julio.

"And we're heroes, too. Legacy and me, we had a plan to clean Vegas' drug problem, too. We thought you were going to be a threat to that, but now I can see you're not. We don't have to fight."

Julio's hand was back to his side. Lady Harrow was completely free, but she had no intention of fleeing or fighting him.

"What was your plan?" he asked. He sounded as though he was choking up, but Harrow couldn't tell if that was just his normal pained speech.

"We were—" she caught herself. She had to reveal to Jenna now that she had been playing her, and the Del Toros, the whole time. But there wasn't any choice. There was no defeating Titan Black. She had to befriend Julio Carillo. "We were going to become the only distributor in the city, and then flood the market with my illusions—imaginary drugs with fake effects. Everyone would believe they were using, but they'd be fooled by their own minds. The coke in circulation would be widespread, but completely fake and harmless without anyone realizing."

Harrow didn't look at Jenna. Legacy did, but her face didn't give away Jenna's reaction.

Black thought for a few moments, taking in the woman standing beneath him.

"That boy," he finally said. "Needs help. Fast. I tried to hold back, but I'm not always in control. Help him, save him for me, hero."

"What?" she asked, taken aback. It sounded like he was leaving, and he turned his back to confirm it.

"I'm leaving." He began walking toward the single garage door. "I'm no hero. I can't be. But you? You could be an inspiration. You've got Vegas covered."

"Where will you go?" Harrow wasn't ready to say goodbye. For some reason, she wanted to stay with Julio, to learn more about him and understand what had happened to him. More importantly, there was the question of the creatures. "And what about the others like you, those zombies in the streets? Their skin is like yours, they have those same eyes!"

He gave out a gruff sigh, as though in concerned acknowledgement. "I thought you said that. I don't know anything about them; I'm not the source of anything. Anyway, I think I need to be alone. I need to find myself, far away from here."

His answer regarding the monsters was unsatisfying and unconvincing, but Harrow needed first to keep him around to press at it more. "Julio, we can find that together if you—"

"Julio is dead." he said again suddenly, turning his head back to her slightly as he reached for the bottom of the large door. "I need to find Titan Black; what *he* means. And you can't help me with that—no one can."

Titan lifted the garage door slowly, careful not to run it off its tracks, revealing himself to the warm Nevada air. He stepped outside, his feet crackling against the older and weakened asphalt. He turned his head back one last time to glance at the three women, but mostly at one in particular. "*Hasta luego*, Lady Harrow."

With no more to say, Black leapt up like a huge projectile, practically flying off into the night sky.

Lady Harrow turned to Legacy and hugged her, but felt the stare of another ally on the back of her head. She released, and turned to see Jenna glaring at her.

"Jenna, I'm so sorry, this—"

"So that was your plan all along, huh?" she said accusingly.

"Hey, you listen here you little—" Legacy said, trying to step between the two before Jenna put up a hand to interrupt.

"You were still gonna make all of us money off of this, right?"

Harrow and Legacy looked at each other before returning to the human. "Uh, yes—yeah, we would have to, to keep up the illusion that nothing had changed." Harrow explained.

"Then we don't have a problem."

"Really?" Legacy asked, clearly surprised and impressed.

"You think I was with the Del Toros 'cause I care about an honest living selling coke?" She smiled.

Lady Harrow couldn't help but smile too, even letting out a small laugh. "No, I guess not. I just figured, you know, there'd be some kind of honor or something involved."

"That's movie bullshit. It's all about money. For me at least. But yeah, I'm totally on board. And if you ladies still are, I've got a good idea what our next move should be. After we get Kicks to a hospital, that is."

"Our?" Legacy asked, making no effort to mask her attitude, but moving with the others toward the boy on the ground.

"We are, yes." Harrow said to Jenna as she nudged Legacy with her elbow. They all knelt down to pick up Kicks. The two alien women took care with his seriously injured legs, putting most of their pressure on his torso to keep him up. Jenna held him by his arms, linking her own up at his chest for support. He was still totally knocked out. "What have you got?"

"One condition." Jenna said, using her finger as a visual aid, though she quickly returned it to its position to maintain her grip of the damaged young man. "You explain what the Hell just happened with all that crazy gun and sword and wall stuff."

Lady Harrow thought for a moment, with a nervous glance to her partner across from her. "Umm, maybe. We'll see."

The human shrugged. "Alright, good enough. Let's get going."

The three woman stepped out of the open garage door and moved around to the other side of the building, gently loading Kicks into the back seat of Harrow's sedan, his head on Jenna's lap.

Issue 11
The Finished Score

For as much time as she spent there, there were few places Lady Harrow hated being more than on the Las Vegas Strip.

It wasn't just that she wasn't terribly interested in gambling—especially games that she couldn't fix, like slot machines—or that the food and atmosphere were rarely as impressive as they pretended to be—although that was true of anywhere, but it was especially prominent here to her, being well-practiced in making things appear as they are not. Her main issue was the people. If they weren't ignorant, drunk, or both, then they were arrogant and nauseating in their personalities; entitled and uppity. And nowhere were humans more obnoxious than at the Cosmopolitan.

Part of that was a fault of the Cosmopolitan, being the resort most adept at creating an air of superiority. The greatest effort and care had been put in to make the hotel and casino seem like the affluent lounge for the successful it was going for. The whole interior was astounding in its complexity and wealth. The environment invoked a sense of both admiration and envy. Crystal chandeliers hung from every crevice in the ceiling, harsh lights that rivaled the cheap neon popular on the rest of the Strip shone on extravagant marble and tile floors. The furniture was maintained and presented at the highest class. Every space was both warm and inviting, yet somehow also discomforting in its lavish coolness.

Harrow very much did not want to be here.

But, it was necessary. With the Del Toros still struggling to rebuild their lost empire in the wake of Titan Black's gutting, her and Legacy's plans relied on helping Jenna as much as they could. That meant keeping the vestiges of their former criminal rivals from reorganizing. Any disruption was sufficient, but they didn't want to have to constantly babysit washed-up drug lords for the next month. This was the most efficient way to handle all of their problems at once.

Tonight was the public event to announce and celebrate Las Vegas' new energy grid. Although the Strip did not technically fall within the city limits, it was still in the greater Las Vegas area, and would be included in the upgrade.

Evidently, Snow Dynamics Enterprises had recently reached an agreement with NV Energy, and the two had been working together over the past few weeks to prepare their entire operation to switch over to their new clean energy supply. Ordinarily, the transition would have been seamless, but the city wanted to make an event out of it, and so the Cosmopolitan became the stage for a new era to begin at midnight. The City of Lights would shine free and forever after tonight.

Although the party was very much open to the public, many big names of both fame and infamy were here to celebrate and make connections. That included those individuals left over from the main drug rings Harrow and Legacy had spent so much time eliminating. They had been lying low since their respective dissolutions—unwilling and unable to return to the light and resume their business—but times like this made one feel empowered and rejuvenated, ready to take on the world.

110

She couldn't have that.

"I see the Italians." Jenna's voice rang in Harrow's ear. She tapped her earring—a clever disguise for a communication device, allowing the three women to speak even despite the crowded quarters and roaring chatter.

"Where?" Legacy said. Harrow couldn't see her lover, but she glanced back from her current position by the escalator to see where the human might be looking.

Jenna was perched above most of the partygoers, inside the Chandelier, on the second floor of the open bar and lounge. From this vantage point, she had a good eye on most of the guests, though she couldn't see very far into the gaming floors. That meant her marks were in the main space that Harrow currently occupied.

However, Harrow couldn't see Jenna, either. She must have been on the other side of the Chandelier, by the other escalator and the entrance. The Telignen shrugged and returned to her own sweep.

They didn't know who to expect, or when. But they were certainly in the right place. Still, it was a big party, and as they already knew, Jenna could only see so much.

From the chatter ringing in her ear, Harrow could tell that her partners were working to take out the current targets. She wasn't paying attention, somewhat phased out in aimless thought, but by the long sentences back and forth, they had it covered. Once Legacy found them, she would coax them away from the party and bind them, leaving behind a healthy amount of planted evidence for various crimes—a task she was plenty capable of herself.

Lady Harrow couldn't tell for certain whether she was in a trance, or free. Nothing was distracting her or weighing her down;

111

not the party, not the voices in her ear. But at the same time, she wasn't particularly focused on anything. She was absent.

She found herself wandering about, before stepping onto the carpet of the table games floor. She tried to regain control—or was it shake away control? She thought about why she was here, or rather, why it made sense to be here despite not intending to be. As Jenna couldn't see very far into the casino floors, it made sense that these should be swept for any marks, too.

Finding her balance, both mentally and physically, she strutted through the crowded space, weaving between people and tables like a predator. She examined each face at each game, observed every motion. Part of her wanted to mess with the humans throwing their money away by manipulating their cards or dice, but she was on a mission. And besides, there was nothing to gain if she wasn't playing.

Her eyes fell upon an empty table. Only a dealer stood there, politely waiting for a guest to approach. He was tall and burly—he looked too aggressive to be working at a card table. But his firm and weathered face was relaxed, his hands folded neatly on the table. The sign for the name of his game hung a few feet from his short red hair: House Rules.

"You take everyone's money already?" she said as she took a seat at the table, making a casual smile out of her mouth.

"No ma'am." he replied, returning her facial gesture. He tapped the green felt of his table like one would the roof of a car in pride. "Brand new game, no one wants to learn how to play. Or they just don't like it."

"Oh yeah? How's it go?" Harrow asked. She had all night to hunt, and sometimes the best place to search a crowd was from within. And anyway, this table was in the very back of this gaming floor; the dealer faced away from the Chandelier. She had an excellent view of the area before her.

"It's not too hard. Kinda like Blackjack 'cause you play against the dealer. You bet, then you get a hand of three cards." The dealer—she noted his nametag said Daniel—laid out three cards face-up in example: a two of clubs, a king of clubs, and a seven of diamonds. "You can choose to return one of those cards. Generally, you want to try to return a card that's similar to another you already have. Here you've got two clubs, so you'd want to return one of them. Let's say you return the two."

Daniel took the two of clubs before dealing out a replacement card: a three of hearts.

"Then, I lay out the *rule cards*. There's fifteen rules, they're printed here for you." He gestured to the fifteen spaces drawn in yellow on the green table. "If your cards match any of the three rules I lay out, they're dead. You get a payout based on how many cards survive: no cards means you lose your money, one card you break even, two you get one-to-one payout, three is two-to-one."

He slid a card from his second, smaller automatic shuffler onto the table and flipped it up. Then another, and then a third. They matched three of the rules printed on the felt: 2-5, Diamonds, and Highest.

"So with these rules, your whole hand would be dead. 2-5 kills your three, Diamonds kills your seven, and Highest kills the highest card in your hand, including dead cards, which is your king. But as you can see by the list, some cards are harder to kill than others. Faces don't have a group card like 2-5, but can still get hit by the color and suit rules. Aces have their own rule, but they count as low so they can't get hit by the Highest card."

"Interesting. Lotta nuance to it. I see why no one wants to play."

"But there's a lot of strategy, too. That trade-in can really change your whole hand. One last thing, at the start you can make two separate bets: your standard bet for how many cards survive, and an optional joker bet."

"You play this game with jokers?" This was a surprise, and Harrow leaned in, devoting more attention to Daniel's explanation.

"Yep. If you get a joker in your first hand and placed a joker bet, it's four-to-one payout." He smiled at this. Evidently, that statement tended to draw people in. "But, the Joker doesn't count as a surviving card for your standard bet, and you can't trade it. If you don't get a joker in your first hand, you lose the joker bet outright."

"And what if I get two jokers?"

Daniel raised an eyebrow, crossing his arms to stifle a laugh. "Seven-to-one. But that's less than a one percent chance."

"Count me in."

"Alright, go ahead and place your standard, and joker if you want. Fifteen dollar minimum for the standard, no minimum for the joker."

Harrow put down a ten-dollar and five-dollar chip for her standard bet. She decided not to play the joker game until she got the hang of the rules.

Daniel slid three playing cards out from his automatic shuffler and onto the table, flipping them over one at a time for his player's hand. Six of hearts, ace of spades, joker.

Of course she got a joker.

"Joker, no bets." Daniel said as per what Harrow assumed was his script. He slid the face-up joker away and into his stack of used cards.

She eyed her remaining two cards.

The fifteen rules really spread out across the whole deck. Some cards were probably safer than others, but there were certain combinations of rules that were just brutal. If the Red card and Black card were in the same round, no strategy mattered; every card was dead. Odd and Even was almost as cruel, though faces and aces were spared in that case.

Her current hand had a lot going for it. The ace could only be hit by Black, Spades, Lowest, and of course, Ace. The six was dead to 6-9, Red, Hearts, Even, and Highest. It had one more potential killer than the ace, but none of their rules overlapped. Being down a card hurt, but that couldn't be helped.

"No trade." she said simply. She wasn't too invested yet, but her interest was piqued.

He dealt out three rule cards from his shuffler, flipping them over in the middle of the felt table. 2-5, Ten, Red.

"One survivor, break even." He flipped over her six, denoting its status. His words were stale and unimprovised, but he smiled and winked at her reassuringly. "That was the right call. And see that's how the joker bet gets ya. I tell ya, the first time a guy that's already down on his luck gets a joker without making a bet, is the last time."

"Good thing I'm a woman, then." She winked back playfully and kept her minimum bet in play as he collected the cards and prepared to deal a new hand.

One by one, Daniel flipped over her cards. Jack of diamonds, four of clubs, ten of clubs.

"Two clubs again?" she said with some annoyance, though not intending to imply foul play.

"This'll be the last hand for this deck. Next one's shuffled and ready to go." The dealer patted the second automatic shuffler to his left.

"Alright, that's good. Well, I guess I'll trade the… four." Harrow decided as she slid her card toward him. He took it silently, dealing out her replacement: queen of diamonds. "Ouch."

"Good luck to you, ma'am." Daniel said politely as he reached for the automatic shuffler to his right, which had been working on the next deck of fifteen rule cards.

Although it wasn't any different than how he had done it before, it felt like he flipped over each rule card, one by one, agonizingly slow. Harrow's heartbeat waned in anticipation.

Black.

Daniel flipped over her ten in acknowledgement of its death.

Lowest.

Her ten was already dead, but she was still noticeably agitated. Lady Harrow did not like losing, and she was very interested in this new game. There were two cards that broke her hand down to zero—a one-in-seven chance—and those were not odds she favored. A small gathering of two or three people was also starting to form around the table, which only added to her unease.

The dealer reached for the final rule card from the machine on his right and slid it across the table before finally flipping it over.

Odd.

Her jack and queen survived.

"Two survivors, one-to-one payout." he said with only a hint of pride as he picked up a five and ten chip to set in front of his player. He began to collect the cards and return them to their respective homes. Harrow took this opportunity to up her ante, raising her standard bet to twenty-five dollars. She also decided to put a five-dollar chip down for her joker bet.

Daniel smiled knowingly, but evidently this required no scripted acknowledgement. He reached for and began sliding cards from his left. He dealt a card first to the man that Harrow only now realized had sat on her right, then to her, then back to the new player.

He must have overheard the explanation, if not played earlier in the evening, because he already had his standard and joker bets out—fifteen and five respectively—and was eyeing his cards with a stoic poker face.

The man on her right's hand was a queen of diamonds, a seven of diamonds, and an eight of clubs. Lady Harrow had an ace of hearts, an eight of spades, and a five of spades. Neither were in particularly good positions.

"No jokers." Daniel said coldly, reaching for both Harrow's and the man's meager bets. "Any trades, sir?"

It was the man's turn first. He silently slid Daniel his seven of diamonds. The dealer slid him a new card, flipping it over to reveal a ten of hearts.

"I'll trade my ace." Harrow said as she slid the dealer her card.

He hesitated to take it. "You sure?" he asked with a raised eyebrow. It wasn't frowned upon for dealers to politely confirm with players about obviously poor moves in games like Blackjack, and House Rules was no different. And, this was an objectively poor choice; Harrow had two spades. Even if they didn't overlap in any other rules outside of Black, it was still risky to leave them together, and even more so to trade away a card that shared absolutely no qualities with them.

But, she nodded and nudged the card further away from her. Daniel noticeably cringed, but took the ace from her. He reached for the deck to his left to slide a new card over to her, turning it over to complete her hand: a six of clubs.

The dealer reached now to his right, sliding three rule cards along the green felt before flipping them over, one at a time.

Red.

He reached for the man's queen and ten, killing them and leaving him with just one card. He sighed with annoyance, but kept a straight face.

Clubs.

Daniel reached for the man's final card, turning it over and leaving the man's whole hand dead. He stood up, frustrated with his poor luck, leaving behind his lost standard bet for the dealer to scoop up. He then turned to Harrow, flipping over her six.

Then the final card. Again, Harrow was unexpectedly tense, and this wasn't helped by the two women who were now sitting on either side of her, eager to play in the next round.

The dealer flipped over the last rule.

Middle.

Her six was her middle card, already dead. She was left with her eight and her five unscathed.

"Two survivors, one-to-one again." Daniel said with a bit more excitement. He collected her hand and the rule cards before paying her in a twenty and a five chip.

As the two women placed their bets—both with the minimum standard bet, but one with ten on the joker—Harrow contemplated what to do for herself. She was having fun, but it was taking time away from searching for and handling her targets. She had work to do, and couldn't just leave it all to Jenna and Legacy.

But there was time for one more hand. And she would ensure it was a fun one.

Lady Harrow took her standard bet back down to the minimum fifteen, putting the leftover ten and her newly earned twenty-five into her joker bet. She added a further ten dollars for a staggering forty-five dollar bet.

Daniel chuckled at this, but began dealing out the cards anyway.

The woman to her right got a nine of spades.

Harrow received a nine of diamonds.

The dealer flipped over a two of spades for the last player.

Going back around, Daniel gave the first woman a three of diamonds.

He flipped over Harrow's second card to reveal, to his surprise and excitement, the black-and-white joker.

"Wow, lucky lady!" Daniel exclaimed.

"You bet." she said, her relaxed voice betrayed by her devilish grin invading her right cheek.

He turned back to the last player, revealing her second card: a seven of hearts.

Once more, he flipped over a card for the player on Harrow's right: an eight of hearts.

The dealer slid Lady Harrow's card from the shuffler and along the felt table. He wasn't moving any faster or slower than before, but the situation was charged for everyone involved. A small crowd was now eyeing the new game and the women sitting down at it. The anticipation was intense.

Daniel rolled his eyes in wonder and bewilderment as he flipped over her third card. He had to physically take a step back from the sheer astronomical odds that had unfolded before him.

The full-color joker.

Harrow had been dealt *both* jokers.

She kept her hands folded expectantly as the crowd hooted and cheered lightly at the revelation. Daniel smiled wildly, and once he regained himself, returned to his duties and dealt the third woman her last card: the king of hearts.

"Two jokers, seven-to-one odds!" he shouted with glee as he counted out three-hundred and fifteen dollars in chips, sliding them to Lady Harrow. She happily—but not too eagerly—placed them in her pocket.

She didn't pay much attention to the rest of the hand. There was no need to trade as she had only the one card left that could survive, and she didn't care too much if it did. The rules were flipped over, and Daniel denoted the death of her nine, taking her standard bet of fifteen dollars.

She stood up, but not before exchanging some of her chips for a more manageable five-hundred, then thanked the dealer and wished him a good night. He followed suit, and Harrow returned to the space around the Chandelier to continue her work.

As she stepped away, she reminded herself to tie her fake jokers into permanence with her mental landscaping. Eventually, Daniel would come across the real jokers, but if he or his superior looked back at the pile, they needed to believe it was a fault of their systems and not a scam on her part.

It was almost half-past eleven now. The events would be slowing down in preparation for the countdown to the power switch. As Harrow walked back and underneath the balcony Jenna was perched upon, she took note of the collapsible stage. Once the speeches and such began, most people's attention would be diverted; an ideal time to lure away the would-be crime lords.

As there hadn't been any indication of more targets in the past little while, she decided to climb the spiral staircase up from beneath the Chandelier to the second story, inside of it. The strings of crystal fell in waves from above, arcing down and hanging from the edge of the balcony, creating a lavish effect of simultaneous privacy and exhibition.

Harrow crept up from behind Jenna, intending to surprise her. She tapped the sides of her waist, prompting the human to jump and turn around. When her would-be attacker came into view, her look of shock became one of relief, but she still held her hand to her bare sternum in support.

"Jesus, H! I almost fell over the wall!" she exclaimed.

Her glittering silver gown was much more extravagant than Lady Harrow's attire—she had opted for a short-cut dress that did nothing to display her chest, and a somewhat nicer leather jacket than her normal one. Jenna preferred a much longer getup; the sparkles very nearly touched the ground, although they lifted themselves just enough to allow attention to be drawn to her matching heels. Being more open with her body than Harrow, the shining material opened up quite a bit at her cleavage, cutting down to the lowest edge of her bust. The Telignen couldn't imagine enjoying so much attention from humans in that area. Jenna was a unique specimen of mind.

"Sorry, couldn't resist." Harrow said, shrugging with a smile. Jenna socked her lightly in the shoulder, but wasn't any more annoyed than that.

"What are you doing up here?"

"Speeches are about to start, and it sounded a little quiet up here," she replied, pointing to her earring device. "I thought you might be lonely."

"Aw, how sweet. Well let's get Legacy up here, we can watch the festivities together." She tapped her own earring, before speaking to the general air. "Hey L, come on up to the balcony. We're gonna watch the show."

A brief silence. Then, Legacy's voice sounded in Harrow's ear. From her reaction, Jenna was getting it, too. "Why? We've got things to do."

"'Cause we want to. Come on, Harrow's already up here!"

"Alright, I'll be up in a minute."

The two women on the balcony returned to their own conversation while they waited for their associate.

"So did you notice who's actually speaking at this?"

"I would assume Marco Nieve, but I haven't seen him. Maybe just some rando from Snow Dynamics. Probably the mayor, too. Maybe someone from the Cosmopolitan's parent company."

"Ah. Okay. Well they'd better hurry, getting pretty close to twelve, and politicians can talk a lot." Harrow cracked, to the amusement of her human partner.

She felt a hand on her shoulder, and saw another on Jenna's opposite. "Great idea, J!"

Legacy was here.

"I can't believe how dumb these goons are, thinking it'd be safe to come out of hiding here. I've bagged three already!" the Svuarti gloated eagerly. "How's your haul been, *m'lady?*"

"I got a little tied up." she replied with only minor embarrassment as she pulled out the five-hundred dollar chip. "But if we're counting gambling, I think I'm ahead!"

Legacy and Jenna both laughed as they eyeballed the green chip.

"Damn, is that real?"

"Sure is! The cards I used to win it weren't, though."

"That's my girl." Legacy applauded before leaning in to kiss her on the cheek.

"Oh, shush shush, it's starting!" Jenna nudged the two aliens as a woman took to the stage below. They had an excellent vantage point; it was a surprise there weren't more people up here. Of course, gambling was far more important for some people. And anyway, most of the guests this evening were likely only here for the cheaper tables and discount food.

"Thank you all for being here this evening!" the woman proclaimed. She wasn't familiar to Lady Harrow, but none of the people on stage were. Which was probably a good thing, for them. "As many of you know, I'm Las Vegas' mayor Krista Laine, and I'm here to introduce our special guests this evening in celebration for our power grid transfer. At midnight tonight, Las Vegas and the rest of the area provided by NV Energy will become completely green and require significantly less money to use and maintain! I won't take up too much time here—"

"That's a surprise." Legacy chuckled.

"—so please, allow me to introduce miss Michelle Ramirez!" the mayor paused and gestured to the other woman behind her, who stood in preparation for having the microphone turned over to her. "As the Chief Operating Officer for Snow Dynamics Enterprises, Michelle and her team have been working closely with the city and our energy provider to transition the power grid over to their new system. Without further adieu, I'll pass the mic over to her and let her take it away!"

Mayor Laine handed the microphone to Ms. Ramirez, shaking her hand before taking her seat behind the new speaker.

"Hello Las Vegas!" she said, taking only a beat to pause. "I apologize, I'm sure many of you were hoping to meet the hero Shatterbug tonight. Mister Nieve sends his apologies for having to miss this historic event—which he has taken great pride in helping us to see through—but unfortunately an urgent situation has developed that required his unique attention. However, I have something very exciting for you this evening.

124

"How many people know about marconium?" she asked the crowd. Most people were mulling about and not paying great attention to the stage. Of the few dozen that were, maybe a third raised their hands hesitantly. "Alright, that's okay, I figured that. We're still a pretty new company and working in a different state.

"So marconium, which I've got an example of right here," Michelle held up a metal-and-glass cylinder, letting those few who could strain their eyes enough to see the strange but unappealing rock contained inside investigate as much as they could. "Is a mineral discovered buried deep in the Arctic Circle. It has a number of properties that work together to allow us to derive huge amounts of energy from it, using special batteries like this one. These tiny samples last for millions of years, and their output rivals whole nuclear power plants.

"We've arranged with NV Energy to have their power grid—which has already been refitted to work with the new system—be switched over from their current plants to seven marconium power cells at exactly midnight tonight. If all goes according to plan, you won't even notice a difference. At least, until you get your next electricity bill. Because as part of our conditions for providing the resources for this project, your power company will be lowering the cost significantly to all of their consumers under this new grid!"

This garnered some applause from the group, which had grown somewhat now. Michelle waited patiently—and in fact, appreciatively—for the cheers to subside. She set the small battery on the podium before continuing.

"On behalf of Snow Dynamics Enterprises, I'd like to take this moment to express our thanks to Mayor Laine and the city of Las Vegas, and to all of you, for working together to create a brighter future under—"

A collective scream from the lobby entrance behind the stage cut the businesswoman off. She and the rest of the speakers crooked their necks in an attempt to see the source, but a pillar was in their way; as it was in the way of Lady Harrow, Legacy, and Jenna's vision. The edges of the gathering in front of the stage peeked around the corner to get a glimpse of the commotion.

It didn't take long before the source came into view, and the assemblage dispersed in terror. The screaming was now coming from all around, the horrific shrieks conjoined in sound with the pattering of hundreds of feet upon the marble floor, all of it echoing about the expansive room. Jenna's hand squeezed Harrow's as the crystals hanging in front of them shook with the agitated air. Everyone was running, but without a destination. It was chaos. All anyone could think was to run from *them*; those things which had burst through the glass doors and rushed into the lobby; those creatures which hurtled over cowering men and brushed against fleeing women, passing and running around them with impossible fervor; those horrors whose eyes shone nothingness.

The zombies had breached the Cosmopolitan.

Dozens of them, maybe hundreds. They just kept flooding in from the outside.

Lady Harrow wouldn't stay frozen for long. This was the time to act.

She leapt from the balcony, brushing aside the dangling crystals of the Chandelier. She summoned steps beneath her feet as she ran down imaginary stairs, hopping from platform to platform over the horrors' heads.

Jenna opted not to stand idly by, either. She reached into her sparkling silver purse to retrieve her concealable pistol and began to open fire on the monsters. Harrow didn't look back, but she silently hoped the human was a better shot than she pretended to be herself.

The Telignen made way for the stage. This many of them all at once, in one place, so public and open as this; they were after something available only here. They were scavengers, after all. And there was only one thing different about tonight than any other. If Michelle Ramirez spoke the truth, it was reasonable to assume they were after the marconium.

Naturally, Ms. Ramirez had grabbed the battery immediately upon realizing the danger of the situation, but she had nowhere to turn. The sea of rotting flesh was surrounding the stage, and her island was shrinking.

Inexplicably, Harrow's foot felt like it had caught on something. She tripped, and although her focus was unbroken, the illusion beneath her feet shattered. She fell, dazed, into the mess of tangled undead.

They weren't harming her, though. They weren't attacking anyone. They only crowded around the stage; it even appeared as though they were making room for the trapped people to flee from their enclosure. All but the woman carrying the battery.

Lady Harrow wouldn't grant them the same dignity.

She conjured a long, slender blade in each of her hands and began to mow down the herd. She swung the twin swords around her head with ease and finesse—a simple feat when one's weapons happen to weigh nothing and have no air resistance. She slashed at the chests and necks and heads of the creatures, who grasped at each other, all still facing away from her, towards the woman left alone on the stage. They continued to converge on her, despite the alien woman's assault.

She heard whizzing bullets flying past her ears, and saw them reach their marks: the heads of the swarming monsters. Jenna was providing what aid she could, although the horrors barely registered their combined efforts.

Indeed, Harrow's attacks were doing nothing. The creatures hardly seemed to react. Their grey skin parted and allowed her blade passage, but as it slid through their decayed and empty corpses, they did not cease their scrounging for advancement. The scars left behind were dark, but stringy and incomplete. An imperfect darkness; strong enough to survive the blow—if one could call it survival—but still too weak to deflect it, or better, to break the spell.

But they were weak, and that was all Harrow had to focus on. She continued her unrelenting swings, waving the twin blades all about in an attempt for any kind of foothold against the encroaching army. She summoned illusions of more bullets all around Jenna so that she could continue her covering fire; Harrow didn't need to understand firearms to imagine functional pieces of metal and gunpowder, and so she tied their permanence to her tight dress for extra support, which was now ripped slightly with the ensuing action. She was wading through them, getting closer to the terrified woman. The zombies were stupid and animalistic; they clawed at each other, crawling over one another in an attempt to get closer, which only slowed their progress as they fell and tripped. But they *were* making progress.

Again and again, the illusory swords sliced through the greyed skin and black sinews of the menacing horde as a rain of bullets fell upon their heads, squarely in the backs of their craniums. After enough of a battering, or perhaps with enough critical strikes in just the right places, she could bring one down. And this was buying her precious time.

Because, now under true threat, some of the monsters began to turn towards her, leaping at the woman who they now realized could dispatch them. Their howling mouths gnawed and gashed at air as their rotting hands swiped this way and that. Anything they could do to overwhelm their adversary. They weren't working as a team, but in such great numbers, a communal strength was only natural.

But by drawing even a few of them from the stage, she granted the rest more freedom of motion. Finally, three of the zombies which maintained their initial mission were able to clamber up and onto the stage. Harrow watched in horror as one of them swiped at the hand of the woman now crouched on the ground in fear. She retracted her grip out of pain, letting the glass cylinder fall out of her hand and roll onto the stage. Another picked it up without any semblance of care, and the three began running for the door they had entered from with their hobbled, uneasy gait.

The others followed suit. What monsters had yet to be brought down by Harrow's and Jenna's barrage of false metal joined in the retreat. They fled with the marconium in hand, just as quickly and horrifically as they had arrived. They had what they came for. She had failed.

She lowered her arms, resigning herself and allowing her illusions to dissipate. The sword handles vanished, and the thin blades fell to the marble floor, dissolving into clouds of dust upon impact. There was no sound but for the low hum of the lobby music, still playing idly in the empty room like nothing had happened.

Harrow turned around. She looked up at the balcony, but couldn't see Jenna or Legacy. Before she started her search for them, though, she returned her attention to the woman on the stage.

"Are you hurt?" she shouted. There was only a ten foot distance between them, but she expected her voice to carry much less than it did. The echoes of her words resounded on the glass and marble of the deserted Cosmopolitan.

"I— I think so." the woman sobbed, standing up courageously. "They... they took it."

"I know. It's okay. I'm going to find them, and I'll get it back."

"R'Bec!" a voice sounded from behind her. Again, Harrow turned around.

Descending the final steps from the second floor of the Chandelier and walking towards her was Legacy. And she was not alone. For in her arms, with blood staining the left side of her dress, dripping from her opened neck and the splattering on her chin, was a limp and twisted-faced Jenna.

"No."

There was nothing else she could say in that moment.

"No, no, no! I refuse, stop it! Put her down, help her!" Harrow was screaming at Legacy as tears welled in her eyes. Her lover did as instructed, a solemnity in her eyes as she silently laid the human on the ground.

Harrow knelt down beside her associate. She wasn't entirely sure why she was crying. Here before her was a dead human. It was nothing special. She didn't love it, she barely knew it. Was it because it was in her care?

No. It was because she *did* like her. She *was* special to her. She *knew* her, as a friend and as a partner. They were a team, the three of them. But she was human: fragile and weak. And Harrow let her down. And now Jenna was dead. And she was crying over a human.

"There's nothing we can do, R'Bec." Legacy tried to console her, setting a loving hand on her shoulder. "When they decided to attack, a few ran up the stairs. They were so fast and strong, and I didn't have a weapon. I got between them, but they didn't want me. They just... pushed me aside, and did this."

Harrow didn't say anything.

"I'm sorry, R'Bec."

"Stop it, Jieadea." she replied shortly.

"Okay, sorry." From her tone, Legacy wasn't offended. She understood her pain.

They sat in silence there in the empty resort lobby, surrounded by overturned stools, broken glass, abandoned poker chips and scattered cards and dice. They waited over the dead human for Lady Harrow's sobbing to subside.

Issue 12
What Raging Fire

"We're going after them."

"How? And why? R'Bec, think about this."

"I have thought, Jieadea." Harrow said firmly. "This is what we have to do. They were the goal from the beginning. We knew they were a problem, we knew this would escalate, and now it has. And someone is dead. And they got hold of something actually dangerous. No more games, no more other responsibilities or backup plans. We're going after them and ending this. Tonight."

Only now did Lady Harrow look up from Jenna's bleeding neck. She stared right into Legacy's eyes, putting on display the sincerity of her words.

Legacy was unfazed.

"They're a waste of time. There's no reason to go after them; they're not causing any harm or hurting anyone."

"You call this not hurting people?!" she shouted at the Svuarti. "*You* weren't hurting people, you didn't help *at all* and so they killed her!"

Legacy sighed. "She attacked them. No one else is dead; they didn't pay them any attention. They took the battery, but it

132

was just an example. The power grid'll change over safely and fine. In fact… it already has; it's 12:07."

There were too many things fuming through her head to be able to create any kind of coherent response right away. This was about more than what the creatures were or weren't doing; whether they were or weren't a threat. This was about doing the right thing. Striving to be better—to do better.

She hated to admit it, but all this time, Harrow's actions had been selfish. The elimination of drugs in Las Vegas wasn't for the good of the city at all. It was only out of her self-righteousness— her feigned superiority over humanity and their stupid, ignorant vices—that she wanted to outdo them. So that she wouldn't have to look at it or smell it or subconsciously *know* that it was happening in the dark and abandoned corners of her home. There was never any real purpose; never any nobility in her goal. Harrow hardly knew why she had even begun with the Menteur anymore. She had been a fraud.

But this was a chance to be something good—to do something right and make up for her pointless schemes of the past. She didn't know what the zombies were doing. She recognized that they weren't attacking people unprovoked, but they were clearly capable of it, and they created a true sense of terror in the city. They *were* evil.

Lady Harrow had been casting illusions all her life. Creating false employers and brokering deals with imaginary riches; she had made a living of lying to everyone, but her greatest con was aimed at herself.

Lady Harrow was an illusion, not only to her contacts but to her own mind. She didn't exist. The real Harrow—the real R'Bec— was better than this. She was a proud Telignen, someone who wouldn't justify her actions with pretense and metaphor. Someone

133

who wouldn't do the wrong things, even for the right reasons. Not anymore.

"I'm sorry, Jieadea." She stood up, beginning to turn away, towards the entrance. "But if you're not going to help me, then it's the end of the line. I can't keep on being the secret drug trafficker, getting rich off letting people think they're getting high. The zombies aren't a waste of time, the Menteur is. Julio was right, I'm not a hero. But I can be. He's searching for Titan Black—finding what it means to be who he's become—but it's time for me to embrace R'Bec, and become what I lost."

As she began to walk away, a hand fell on her shoulder. She stopped, and tilted her head just enough to glance behind her with the corner of her eye.

"No," Legacy said. R'Bec thought to turn back and keep moving, but her lover's hand tightened. She wasn't finished. "*I'm sorry. You're right.* We'll handle the monsters, because it's the right thing to do. Not like these humans can do it themselves. And then, when we're done, we'll pick up the pieces here. The right way. We'll finish your original goal the R'Bec way. Because I love you, you alien jerk."

Another hand on R'Bec's shoulder allowed Legacy to turn her around. The Svuarti hugged her tightly, to her surprise at first. But shortly, she leaned into it, happy that her friend had come around. Legacy loosened her grip some, allowing space for their lips to meet, alone in the great shining space.

They became suddenly aware that they were not alone, though. Jenna's body was still on the floor. They parted, and R'Bec took Legacy's hand, guiding her to one of the other side doors upon noticing the streaks of flashing lights invading on the marble floor.

Information outside the Cosmopolitan was scarce. It had only been a bit over half-an-hour since the attack on the festivities, and yet it seemed like every cop in the city was parked in and around the resort. Las Vegas Boulevard was all-but-closed, and policemen from every department and division were lending what assistance they could with local security officials.

This wasn't Detective Wallace's field of expertise, although he knew the general protocol for this kind of situation. Still, he left the order-giving to his more familiarized colleagues. At the moment, he was standing idly, making himself available to those running the show but remaining useful by guiding what guests and tourists were still mulling about away from the area.

He saw Victor coming up in his peripheral vision, two coffees in hand. "Thirsty, Colt?"

"No, but I am tired." he replied, taking Officer Levin's offered cup. "Thanks, Vic."

"You got it. Any news?"

"Just sitting tight for now. They've got eyes on the crowd responsible, but holding down the fort here is priority one right now, for most of us."

"Yeah, makes sense." The younger Officer took a long swig of his caffeinated drink. "Wish there was more we could do, though."

"Even if they wanted us to—which they don't—do you think it's a good idea? You've heard the whispers from some of the statements, right?" The Detective sipped delicately from his warm cup.

"There's no way they're true, c'mon, Colt. It was a Vegas party, no one was in their right mind." Victor answered confidently. And yet a crack in his voice and shift in his eyes told Colton that the young Officer was more concerned than he would let on.

"Yeah, well we'll see. Maybe we'll get lucky and they'll throw us a lead. For now, though, we follow orders."

Officer Levin was clearly disappointed in his mentor's resignation, but he was still his superior, and so he'd respect the decision. He stood a few feet aside to cover more space, directing passersby past the building and onto the Fountains of Bellagio.

Wallace turned to look at his friend and partner, and noticed behind him the approach of a policewoman. Judging from her attire, anyway: a respectable grey suit and blue tie, with a standard issue walkie-talkie on her hip. It was a bit breezy, and he imagined that she was grateful she'd chosen to wear pants this evening, rather than a skirt.

"Detective." she said firmly. "My radio's dying, any messages for me?"

"It's been quiet for a few minutes. Sorry, ma'am, who are you?" She was clearly a Detective—no introduction required—but he didn't recognize her bronze skin or curly brown hair. Probably from a different station, and definitely not in narcotics.

"Damn, alright." She flashed her badge from inside her jacket pocket, but the flashing lights from all the vehicles were too bright to warrant any attempt at squinting to read it. "Detective Lucia Fey. I'm waiting to hear back on intel about where the suspects are. Thank you, Detective."

"Oh, ah, Detective!" Victor interjected politely, before she had a chance to turn around all the way. As he jogged over, she turned to face the Officer. "There was just a call about that; they were heading northwest on..."

"On 95." Colton finished as his partner trailed off.

"Do we know where they're headed, yet?" Detective Fey asked, taking her walkie-talkie and tapping it idly in the hopes it would suddenly speak for her.

"No, they're just running, incredibly fast. Unclear how many, they're estimating at least fifty."

"That's unbelievable. Alright, well I'll leave you two to it. Really ought to sort out my own radio. Thanks—"

The buzz of Wallace's and Levin's radios cut her off.

"All units be advised: the suspects are boarding a train approximately one mile northeast of Southern Desert Correctional, facing north. We'll continue pursuit on—"

The transmission fell silent. "Damn ancient outdated tech." Levin said as he fiddled with the device on his waist.

"That'll work; thank you again Detective. Officer." She tipped an invisible hat before turning away.

"Should we go with her?" Victor asked once Fey was out of earshot.

"No, Vic." Colton replied, solemnly. "We've got our orders. Don't want to press our luck again so soon."

As Detective Lucia Fey turned back into the parking garage on the side of the building and rounded the corner up the ramp to where she had parked her black sedan, away from the police convoy, she became aware that she was now alone. There was no one around to observe her.

She pressed her back against a small pillar, a blind spot away from any cameras, and let her illusion dissolve. Her hair began to flatten and fall, becoming a cloud around her head before vanishing into dust, revealing her true hair underneath, which lay straight and close to her neck, the dark red highlighted by her bronze skin. That too began to crumble away, though. Cracks formed on the surface of her flesh, and the beautiful coloration dissipated to reveal her normal skin tone; not her real skin, of course, but the illusion of a deep brown-and-red that she had lived with all her life.

Finally, R'Bec's imaginary suit dissolved into a black dust, but started to reform itself again as she crafted a new illusion to clothe her. She couldn't well be running around, chasing after zombies in the desert, wearing just a torn black minidress.

She got into her car, greeting Legacy with a firm squeeze of her resting hand. "Got it. We're going to jail."

Issue 13
Spellbroken

R'Bec looked out in wonder at the expanse of desert moving quickly before her eyes. It was technically morning now, about 3:15 AM, but the sun was far from reaching over the horizon. This was the twilight. And if she had anything to do with it, the sun would not rise until her enemy was defeated—until the horrors she hunted were purged from her home.

She didn't know how she got so lucky. To find someone to love and to trust in the first place was seemingly astronomical for someone like her. But to find someone who respected her, and cherished her feelings and opinions like Legacy did felt incredible. They had had their disagreements, but they were always able to work them out. And now their partnership was taking them where they had always been headed.

She turned her head to admire her partner standing next to her. She too was looking out the window of the moving train. While R'Bec looked in awe at the dark ground and mountains reaching up at the edge of the sky, Legacy looked up, into the stars. They were still close enough to civilization that the space above was mostly void. But some stars were visible; not nearly as many as on their first night together, but enough to sparkle overhead.

The Svuarti looked so beautiful in that moment. Even with the body—the face—of a human, she was breathtaking. The affection R'Bec had for Legacy's heart and mind made her form more attractive to her. She almost forgot that her body *was* that of a human, and silently hoped Legacy saw her in the same way.

The Telignen took a step back and over, standing behind Legacy. She only now realized that her partner was several inches taller than her, but she didn't mind. R'Bec pressed her lips into the back of her neck, prompting a sigh from the woman. Her hands wove their way down Legacy's shirted waist and onto her thighs. She chose to wear pants to the event at the Cosmopolitan, and given the state of R'Bec's own real apparel, she was probably grateful she had. Still, the touch of a lover's fingers on one's legs was enough to elicit yet another deep breath from the alien woman.

Wishing for more intimacy, more closeness, R'Bec let her fingers fall into Legacy's pockets, pinching at the skin through even less fiber, now. When she reached the bottom of the small pouch in her pants, the Svuarti sucked in air quickly and abruptly, as if in alarm.

They both stood frozen.

R'Bec's fingertip had pressed against something small and cold. It wasn't sharp. No, this was rounded, and not metallic. She was scared to examine it further—only the very edge of her middle finger reached the surface of the object.

Legacy was the first to move. She turned around quickly, laying her own hands on R'Bec's waist and looking deep into her eyes. She smiled, but it seemed forced.

In that same motion, R'Bec had reached as far into the pocket as she could, pinched her fingers around the small trinket and pulled it free. Although Legacy was right in front of her, their chests pressed together, she held the item in her open palm. She raised it up so as to see it over her lover's shoulder.

In horror, in realization, her mind flooded with memories.

"Jieadea," she said, an uneasiness in her voice. But that feeling of confusion was slowly being replaced with conviction and betrayal. She choked. "Why do you have my globe?"

In her hand, just as she remembered it, was her lucky charm. The small globe with the misshapen continents made of minerals, encased in a glass-like sphere and bound by a metal circle. The keychain that she had stolen as a child, whose ring had fallen off long ago. The item she tied the permanence of her mental locks to, keeping in place the nightmares she had grown to fear and hate. And it was in Legacy's pocket.

And then she remembered.

For weeks, ever since that *first day* when they had met; whenever R'Bec would reach for her charm in her back pocket, in an attempt to reassure herself that she was safe and all was right, Legacy would stop her. She'd feign compassion, she'd grab her hand and kiss it or embrace her, but she would not let her touch her back pocket. Because her back pocket had been empty for weeks. Legacy had the globe all this time.

Legacy sighed.

"We were doing so well. We did good work, too. Accomplished a lot." she said, closing her eyes and letting go of R'Bec's waist. If she didn't know any better, she would think the Svuarti's mouth had curled into a smirk of relaxed delight.

R'Bec stepped back. And then she remembered.

Whenever R'Bec would show the slightest hint of defiance, or reclaim the smallest gleam of volition, Legacy would reach into her own pocket and grip that globe. And then she would forget. And Legacy would replace that memory—that feeling of hate and

141

fear and disobedience—with love and affection and loyalty. But R'Bec hadn't been loyal. She'd been brainwashed.

"All this time, you had my globe. You've been... You've been using me." Tears welled in R'Bec's eyes.

"I'd like to think we've been using each other. Don't pretend you didn't enjoy it." Her eyes opened in accusation and mirth. Legacy's face was a twisted one. R'Bec almost forgot she was looking at a human face.

She sniffed hard, trying to hold back her sobs. And then she remembered.

All of those tender moments, every kiss, and every love. It was all a lie. It was all Legacy, exploiting and abusing her. She didn't enjoy any of it. It was all pained. The darkest portions of her mind—those pieces that she tied away for fear they would haunt her nightmares—screamed in agony as her conscious mind and body submitted to the will of the Svuarti, dominating her malleable thoughts by manipulating its sentiment for that insignificant stolen globe.

She pushed her hand hard into the middle of Legacy's chest, then turned to run down the train car. Without looking back, she opened the door and stepped outside. Her eyes stung as the rushing warm air pressed her tears back against her face. Not knowing where to go or what to do, she climbed the ladder to her left to get up on top of the train car.

She heard the door slam, and the pattering of hands on metal dowels, indicating that Legacy was following her. She stood at the far end of the moving train car, lit only by the lights peeking from the windows below. Her eyes quickly adjusted to the environment, evening out what visibility she had with the rest of the shadowed desert.

"You're sick, Jieadea! You're a monster! For weeks you made me think this was real! But it never was, was it? I see that now, I remember *everything* now!" R'Bec screamed through croaks and coughs. She struggled to speak through the dry air and deafening screech of the train below, not to mention her emotional turmoil as more memories were rewritten—or more accurately, unwritten—but she didn't care.

"I'm impressed. I've never influenced a Telignen before, but humans don't usually get back what I changed about them." Legacy shouted back. It was easier for her, facing opposite the direction of travel, and the sound carried to R'Bec better than she imagined her own voice was reaching. "To be honest, I didn't think I was gonna be able to affect you at all once I realized what you were. But I held on to that trinket I swiped, just in case. And when I realized I could make you think the way I wanted—Hell, even better than with humans in some ways—well, I could hardly let you go, could I?"

R'Bec was tired of talking. She didn't need to make sense anymore, and she didn't need Legacy's justifications.

She sprinted toward the Svuarti. It was difficult with the wind blowing against her, dragging her back. She thought that one false step might pull her away, but she didn't care. She had to keep moving, she had to beat Legacy.

Her opponent stood motionless. Once R'Bec reached her, she planted her feet and ducked down, aiming a tightened fist for Legacy's stomach.

The alien's dodge was effortless. Keeping one foot in place, she let the other slide back in a circle, arcing her whole body with it. As R'Bec's attack failed but finished following through, making use of all its momentum even against the harsh resistance, Legacy clapped both of her hands onto her arm, twisting it back.

R'Bec nearly lost her footing, but somehow the maneuver also allowed Legacy to hold her more still. Their faces nearly met, and Legacy continued her gloating. "Of course, my control wasn't perfect; you're strong. That's why I love you so much. It just wasn't realistic to change everything about you, nor would I want to. I had to guide you, coax you along the path you were already taking, but in a new direction."

She threw the Telignen's arm—and her body with it—across the length of the roof.

She tumbled a few feet, but caught herself on the emergency hatch in the middle of the car.

"You made me kill that man—James. I didn't wanna kill him; I fought you over and over in my head. But you forced me to! And you made me believe it was right, even after I tried to run from you! You twisted bitch!"

Legacy shrugged. "Another example of why I had to be careful. You weren't supposed to think or fight me. That was a test of how much I'd broken you, but I'd barely scratched the surface."

The Telignen stood up, confidence holding her in place. She gathered all her will to conjure an illusion of her trusty pistol—the same weapon that had killed James. And this one, this bullet meant for Legacy, would be just as real, and just as lethal.

She aimed and fired. Explosion after explosion popped at the hammer. Round after round appeared at the edge of the chamber, letting out streams of bullets toward her opponent. Wind resistance didn't matter when the ammunition wasn't real.

"R'Bec." Legacy said. It was still dark, but she was sure her aim was true. Yet the Svuarti stood there unfazed. "You don't wanna do this."

"Screw you 'I don't wanna do this!'" She didn't understand why her bullets weren't hitting, but she would make them.

Another identical gun materialized in her other hand, and R'Bec once again let out a barrage of illusions to bear down on the cruel alien brainwasher.

"Stop it, R'Bec."

Again, Legacy was unharmed. Unflinching. How?

"Humph. I'm surprised that worked. But then again, I'm *really* not."

"What are you doing, Jieadea?" R'Bec readied herself for another attack, but held her fire to sort out the error in her aim.

"Controlling you, very minutely."

"You can't! I have my globe back!" But even despite this, R'Bec didn't believe Legacy was lying.

"My power works as long as I possess something sentimental to you. I *stole* your globe, but you *gave* me your name."

R'Bec's eyes widened and the bridge of her nose clinched. Her arms shook in anger. She dropped her weapons—letting them dissolve into the warm, dark air—and again charged for the Svuarti.

"It's not as good as your stupid ball," Legacy continued, parrying another of her opponent's punches and landing her own in R'Bec's side. "But it's just important enough to you that I can make you dissolve your smaller illusions."

"Then I'll just beat you *mano a mano*!" she shouted, trying to reach her fists into Legacy's side, her ribs, her shoulder, her chin; wherever she could see an opening.

"You're a magician, R'Bec. I'm a much better fighter. We can tango all night, or you can give me *my* globe back." Legacy landed a balled fist into R'Bec's jaw, causing her to recoil onto the ground.

The Svuarti stood over her. "I'm not gonna be your slave, *ever* again!" she screamed as Legacy gripped her hair and laid her other fist into the Telignen's face, over and over.

"We were happy, hun. We were making a difference—we made something beautiful." The smile on her face was betrayed by the beating she was delivering to the woman beneath her.

"You raped me! You clouded my head and broke inside to do what you wanted!"

"Whatever you wanna call it. It's the best a Telignen is getting on this stinking rock." She let go, letting R'Bec's head fall onto the hard metal cover of the train. "Give up, R'Bec."

Even despite the beating, R'Bec got up quickly. As she did so, she summoned a small army; eleven illusions, all duplicates of herself, rose with her, all sprouting out from her so as to confuse the woman they now surrounded.

"You can't break these magic tricks, Jieadea? Too big?" She had one of her illusions spring forward, turning at the last moment to lay a swinging kick into Legacy.

"Yeah, too big." she replied plainly. She arched her body beneath the swing. But, while still hunched over, she turned around to come face-to-face with the real Telignen. She swung her leg beneath R'Bec's feet, tripping her and causing her to fall.

146

R'Bec rolled to catch herself and control her momentum again, falling off the side of the car.

But the ladder she had climbed up from, between this car and the next, was there to save her. She climbed back up, but the copies had already dissolved. Her loss of balance broke her concentration.

Legacy stood proudly in the middle of the train, waiting for R'Bec's next move.

She once again created two illusions of her favorite pistols, but with significantly bigger barrels. She would test the limits of Legacy's ability to destroy her fantasies.

She fired.

"R'Bec."

She took a step forward, and fired again.

"R'Bec, really."

Another step forward, and two shots this time.

"Stop, R'Bec."

But she didn't stop. She continued to walk forward, closer and closer to the alien downwind of her. Never letting up her barrage of bullets, creating larger and larger rounds each time, trying to find the line. Legacy took a step back, evidently unsure herself of the limit to her control.

"I mean it, R'Bec. It's over."

Finally, the Telignen was within reaching distance.

Legacy reached for her gun. She easily twisted R'Bec's wrist and disarmed her. The oversized pistol fell onto the metal train car and broke into dust and debris before vanishing.

Again, Legacy used this position to bring their faces closer together, then threw her back.

She caught herself in the fall, rolling to regain control on the moving train. She was low to the ground, struggling to get back up with the heavy wind billowing over her, pressing against her and holding her down.

Legacy approached, and kicked her side.

R'Bec recoiled in pain, the sudden shock lifting her slightly from the roof, just enough to slide and turn her on the metal. Her head now hung over the side of the train. No ladder to save her this time; only the dark Sonora desert, fifteen feet below and far too many miles too fast.

Legacy lifted her foot again. She carefully angled it over R'Bec's head. She was going to smash her face and throw her off the train!

The Svuarti's foot began to descend.

As it did, a smile crept on R'Bec's face, before it began to fall backward. Her whole mouth fell into her head, as the dust beneath it dissolved. Her eyes followed, vanishing into a cloud of smoke before her whole head collapsed, falling off the moving train with a puff of illusory smoke, and then becoming nothing.

Legacy's eyes widened in horror and realization, but it was too late to stop herself. Her foot fell, but rather than landing on the face that was no longer there, it passed through the open air, and off the train.

She had put all of her weight into that action, and so the sudden lack of footfall where her mind had told her there should have been caused Legacy's whole body to lunge forward. She screamed as her feeble human form collapsed, whistling through the warm night air. The sound of her body hitting the ground—of her bones snapping and her squishy flesh splattering on the desert earth—were inaudible next to the roar of the moving train.

When R'Bec peaked her real head back up and over the ladder, Legacy was long gone. The top of the train was empty; even the last of her illusory doppelganger was fully dissolved back into the air without even a lingering dust particle.

She returned to the comfort of the inside of the train.

What was she doing here? She had come here with Legacy to finish what they started together. Instead, she discovered the truth of their relationship, and was forced to confront the harsh realization that she had not been in control for weeks. R'Bec had already faced one crisis of conscience—one journey of self-discovery—tonight. Now she had to come to terms with a second.

At least, she would not have to struggle with the loss of another friend. Jieadea—no, Legacy—was never her friend. She was a manipulator, an abuser. She was glad she was dead.

She reached into her pocket for the lucky charm, pulling it out to examine it and to seek its reassuring aura in this time of internal conflict.

The ring was broken.

The metal disc around the outside, within which the globe itself was circumscribed, had a chip broken out of it. It must have been damaged when she was thrown from the roof, before she sent the duplicate up to finish Legacy off. She tried to fish around in her pocket for the other piece, but it was no use. It was gone.

She collected her thoughts in haste, gathering all of her synapses to work in tandem. She sought out the bindings latched around the globe that kept her nightmares in check.

They were gone.

The phylactery was damaged. Her nightmares were free, and they would be invading on her mind—her reality—soon.

It had taken her hours to set those threads in her mental landscape. As she looked out the window, she saw the train was slowing down now. The conductor that—with subtle convincing from Legacy—agreed to take them along the track the zombies' train had travelled was preparing to stop. She was approaching her destination; she didn't have hours.

She reached for her phone and opened up her maps application. Hopefully, the sudden stopping meant their destination was nearing, rather than just a simple station. If her targets were heading somewhere specific, it was possible it would be marked, and close.

There was only one thing of note nearby. It couldn't be a coincidence; the track she evidently travelled upon wasn't marked—they must have separated from the real line some time ago. The creatures could have stopped their train in the middle of the journey along this unmarked route, and walked the rest of the way. That had to be it; there was no better explanation.

A few miles to the west, with as much detail obfuscated as possible, was the military installment officially known as Groom Lake.

No globe to protect her. R'Bec was going to have to make the trek through her mind as well as the desert. Her nightmares would be haunting her as she made way in pursuit of the zombies, and towards Area 51.

Issue 14
Games of Make-believe

Colton didn't know how he let his subordinate talk him into this.

"We gotta make up for ourselves, Colt!" Victor had said. "We can hop on one of the helicopters going after them. I'm sure they won't say no to extra eyes on a manhunt like this."

He was right, of course. But that didn't mean they should be there. Yet here they were, on a helicopter out into the desert at 3:30 in the morning. Not strictly disobeying orders, but certainly going out of their way to not follow them.

Still, he couldn't deny that his pride had been hurt since they failed to take down Lady Harrow and her associate. He needed a win—for himself would be ideal, but just to assist the whole force in a victory would be more than enough.

It was deafening in the air, and Wallace was blind at this time of night. The searchlights were of little help to him, but he imagined the pilots had better eyes than he—and actual equipment. The Detective could only just make out a voice coming through his enormous headphones over the roar of the turbines.

"Suspicious activity spotted, prepare for descent." was the gist of it. A lot of it was cut out by Wallace's old ears, but the eagerness on Officer Levin's face across from him told Colton that he'd interpreted the buzzing in his head correctly.

The hovering machine was brought down slowly—as best he could tell in the dark, anyway—but touchdown still caused the unfamiliar passengers to jerk. As the rotors began to slow, the police and other law enforcement agents exited the tiny capsule, ducking their heads as they hopped onto the dusty ground one after the other.

Two other choppers had made the trip, allowing for considerably more visibility. A total of twelve men and women now huddled together against the dark.

Detective Wallace first noticed the train. It was modern, of course, but its age was starting to show. Clearly abandoned; he wondered how the reported individuals had managed to conduct it out here, and to stop it safely.

"Alright, we'll set this up as our base of operations." One of the women from another of the helicopters was clearly taking charge. She wore more of an office-like attire, but her blue jacket gave away her status as an FBI agent. Good to see the federal government lending a hand for once, even if it took a crisis to get their attention. Still, the fanfare told Wallace that this was probably being treated as a terrorist attack, and he wondered if they were prepared for such a task. "We've got more volunteers on their way on the ground, but we're the first responders. Me and my team will get started here in setting up for the arrivals.

"I want... you three," she pointed to one of the men from Colton's helicopter, who was standing beside two women from the third. "To explore the train here. Treat it as a crime scene, get to know it before forensics gets onsite. The rest of you, start fanning out. Trampled dirt and vegetation here shows they're heading *that* direction. We'll use local law enforcement radios to keep in touch. What channel?"

She looked directly at Detective Wallace.

"Uh, one should be fine. Won't be any interference out here." he replied quickly. He felt a little embarrassed being caught off-guard, but he thought he had seen something behind the leading agent, out in the direction he and Victor were about to journey.

"Okay, stay close to each other and don't get too adventurous out there. We'll have plenty more coming to search the area more efficiently; we all wanna get a head start here and be the heroes, but I don't wanna have to lead two search parties."

With that, the group divided into their designated tasks. Victor grabbed a flashlight from the now-open supply crate and passed it to Colton, before grabbing another for himself. They met with the other three of their team—two more women from the LVPD, and an FBI agent apparently separate from the crew leading the base camp.

"Alright, let's start fanning out." the agent started, clearly just as willing to take charge where he could. "Keep the choppers in sight behind you for now, and for God's sake don't lose sight of each other."

The four police officers looked at him, but started to turn anyway into the desert. As much as Wallace didn't want to admit it—for fear of bolstering the man's ego—his directions were the correct procedure, although the four of them already prepared with that exact plan in their heads.

Detective Wallace and Officer Levin stayed fairly close to each other as they pressed through the encroaching darkness, never more than a few dozen feet from one another. Colton thought to himself that they should probably be spreading out to cover more ground, but he wasn't terribly optimistic they were going to find much so close to the train. The people behind this attack took the railways and stopped here for a reason, but if their destination wasn't obvious right at the site, it was likely some ways away. Technically it could just be concealed, but even then it would be near impossible to locate without proper equipment, and almost certainly not until morning.

Although, there was the question of what he had seen behind the lead agent, out here in the wasteland. Something moved, very clearly to him even despite that darkness, though it was only a glimmer. There was no wind tonight, and nothing to reflect the lights from the landing zone—and even those lights didn't match the flash of purple he thought he had seen. But if something was indeed out here, he would rather his partner close by. Just in case.

"Hey, Colt." Levin whispered through the warm air.

Wallace inhaled quickly at the surprise, instinctively holding in the dry breath, before exhaling. "What?" he said with a clear tone of annoyance.

"You notice those tracks, too?"

"The what?" Wallace replied, ensuring he'd heard right. Of course, he *had* noticed—almost right when they landed. But Victor must have thought he didn't know what he was talking about, and so continued.

"The railroad tracks. They were new, laid down recently. Haphazardly."

"Yeah, yeah I noticed. They've been planning this for a long while." Wallace shone his light slightly in Levin's direction. He tried to tell himself it wasn't to check on his partner, but there was little reason to search the few feet between them quite so thoroughly.

"Lends some to the terrorist theory they're obviously playing with. You think they caught it, too?" Victor stopped now to gauge his superior's reply, and whether he'd gone too far.

Colton paused at this, choosing his words carefully. "If they didn't right away, they will once they take a look around. It stands out pretty well."

"Yeah, you're right."

A few more moments of silence was evidently too much for Officer Levin to bare, as it wasn't long before he brought up a new topic of discussion.

"What do you think we're looking for?"

"The group that attacked the Cosmopolitan." Detective Wallace knew what his partner was trying to get out of him, but he wasn't sure he was ready to hear himself speak those words.

"You know what I mean, Colt." Again, Victor stopped for a moment. He was taking this seriously. Perhaps Colton needed to, as well.

"Sorry." he answered after a moment, taking another to pause and again choose his words. "I don't know. Probably terrorists, I'm sure the FBI has a pretty good idea of what they're charging into."

"And what if they don't?" Victor said, only now raising his voice. Wallace turned to him now, shining his flashlight at his respected subordinate. "What if the people at the party were right? They couldn't all be drunk and high enough to all see that, much less the same thing. You heard some of those statements, you must've."

Colton shook his head. He was by no means an old man. But he had seen a lot in all his years of law enforcement. He had a pretty good idea of what was possible, and what the mind was able to imagine.

And he was stubborn. Not one to believe what he couldn't see, what didn't match his idea of reality. The notion that there could be actual zombies in the world was asinine. And the idea that any rational person could believe in such a thing was obscene to him.

But he respected Victor Levin. He knew him to not be a fool. So for once in his life, he thought it might be time to ease his preconceptions and consider the young man's points.

And he did have points. There were valid concerns. How did so many people come to the consensus that they all saw the same thing? They ran in different directions, and it wasn't like this was some planned mass-pranking of law enforcement. There was a body, after all, and a missing piece of powerful technology. A serious crime took place, and everyone just decided to blame it on the boogie man? No, at the very least they *believed* they saw something.

Which lead to Lady Harrow. The woman who made Colton believe golf clubs had fallen in front of him, that golf balls covered the floor beneath his feet. And they had felt so real, too. He could *feel* the ball rolling under him; his body jerked and flew in a way that couldn't be facilitated by a trick of the light. He already had experience with seeing something that before he could never believe. What was another?

157

And after all, it may very well be the same thing. The theft and murder didn't seem to match the Menteur enforcer's *modus operandi*, but several individuals with ties to gang and drug activity were found already restrained at the scene. That was pretty good evidence that Harrow had been there. How did it all fit together? And again, the railroad tracks didn't match her established behavior.

Wallace had been lost in thought, so he wasn't sure how long it had been since he turned to acknowledge the Officer. He drew his attention back through his eyes and looked to Levin again, preparing to apologize and share his conclusions.

But before he could let out a breath, Victor's face turned to one of horror as his hand rose to point behind the Detective.

Some force shifted through the darkness just outside of Wallace's peripheral vision, crashing into him and sending him to the ground some ten feet away.

True to his training, Victor reached for his piece and opened fire on the entity—judging by the sounds piercing the still air of the night—causing Colton to recoil back to the ground, interrupting his attempt to get to his feet.

He counted only five shots before a grunt from the young Officer informed the Detective that he too had been struck. The coarse dirt crunched beneath the sliding weight of the new victim. Only now did Wallace's adrenaline kick in, granting him the strength to roll over and face their attacker.

Some new darkness loomed over them. It was brighter than the lack of light surrounding them in the desert, but it was still a gloomy shade of black. Its outline was made more disparate from the environment by the purple glow radiating from its form. Violet lights shone in seemingly random places all across the creature's body, glowing and dimming without pattern or apparent purpose. But beyond just pulsating, they also seemed to crawl around the dark flesh of the monster. As the Detective shone his flashlight upon it, casting a clear but minimal sheen over the horror's legs and face, he could tell that in fact, the shifting luminescence was within the being, buried just under the surface.

The monster charged, angling its long porcine head down to better allow for its tusks to impale its target. The four hoofed legs did not crunch upon the sand and browned foliage as the two men's bodies did, but rather boomed and howled, like some empty drum thumped through the desert instead of the eight-foot mutant of a boar preparing to prey upon them. This resounding rap was accompanied by the horrific squeals of the beast, like out of some nightmare long forgotten.

There was no training for this. The threat posed to Detective Wallace was otherworldly; he had no idea how to react in this situation. But evidently, his body did. He somehow found the courage to leap to the side with power from both his feet kicking into the rough earth and his hands vaulting him up, even despite the sharp fragments of rock that attempted to pierce his palms.

The oversized hog stopped abruptly, having no difficulty slowing down on the loose pebbles covering the ground beneath its hooves. The lights under its shadowy skin continued their random dance inside the creature, but with their help in differentiating from the lightless surroundings, Colton could still tell that the horror's head had turned to Officer Levin. Wallace stood up, only now finding the strength for it.

"Vic!" he shouted. Now he fell back to his training and instincts, pulling out his own weapon and unloading it into the unfamiliar hide of the beast's backside.

But the assault was not enough. The monster was unfazed by his meager weapon. And Victor was unable to jump far enough out of the way to force his attacker to stop and recollect itself. It turned with ease, hurling its great weight at the Officer rather than plotting to skewer him, as with Colton.

It was by some cursed miracle that Levin survived.

Before the boar reached its mark, the illumination inside it rose suddenly, as the boar was lifted high into the air by a new set of purple flickers that reached its mighty arm around the belly of the beast, pulling it closer to its greater form.

Both policemen watched in horror as the intruding nightmare seemed to swallow their would-be predator whole, greedily stuffing it under its mass with eight huge tentacles. No crunch was heard from the presumed beak of the octopod monster, but instead a terrifying slurping, as though the first beast was reduced to a shadowy, pulsating dust to be sucked up and consumed.

Finishing its appetizer, the gluttonous creature turned its attention—and four of its tentacles—to the gawking two-course meal of Victor and Colton.

"Run!" Wallace shouted at both Levin and his own feet.

He didn't know which direction they were going, but it didn't matter. There were monsters out here—invincible horrors they were ill-equipped to defend against, let alone fight off. They just ran.

The Detective turned back to check on their progress and relative safety. He could see the collection of the octopus' bioluminescence some distance back. Although the lights were clearly moving, the distance between each of those flashing nodes was getting smaller, meeting each other at the edge of Wallace's vision as one massive purple glow. The new monster wasn't chasing them.

But they could not let up. Now that they were some distance ahead, Colton could see that all around him more creatures yet flocked in the barren Sonora. Giant frog-like shapes leapt onto, crushed, and licked up the dust of nightmarish bears and wolves. Three-foot shadows of ants worked as a team to take down magenta lightshows in the shape of hippos and raccoons. A majestic glimmering condor flew down to bury its talons into a horrific sparkling spider, felling the arachnid monster and collapsing it into useless debris.

The brilliant shadowy terrors only became more apparent and populous as they continued, but they couldn't turn back and they couldn't stop. The environment now bent to the creatures, with strings of black and dimming purple arcing between cacti and bushes like webs. Even the ground they feverishly tread on became caked with the slimy—and yet somehow furry, or scaly, or stony—residue. They were obviously getting closer to the source of these horrors, and it was clear to Wallace what that source was.

What wasn't clear to him, immediately, was the banging that sounded as though they were nearing *it*, too. It was metallic, unlike the petrifying noises of the beasts that surrounded and encroached upon them. He couldn't see anything ahead of them but for the flashes of the illusions, which they snaked through with increasing difficulty. Only when they found their path blocked by some new monster feasting upon the dissolving remains of an unreasonably long and wide anaconda did the resounding clanging start to invade upon Colton's ears.

It must have attracted the preying horror's attention too, as the monster started to raise its body up on its titanic hind legs. Its arms—little, relative to the rest of the beast—removed themselves from the decaying shadow of the still-pulsating serpent, and its huge reptilian head came into view. The tyrannosaur arched its neck, parting its mouth to reveal blinking purple teeth. The shadowy dinosaur pointed its snout straight up into the air as it let out its breath.

It was not quite a roar. None of the monsters seemed capable of creating the exact sounds native to the species they imitated. Rather, it was a hollow but thunderous gurgle, echoed by whispered screams and deafened moans. It snarled loudly in the direction of the mysterious sound, ahead of Wallace and Levin, opposite the snake corpse. It hadn't noticed them, but its enormous tail swiped dangerously close to the top of their heads, prompting them to crouch down in fear of being discovered.

Colton glanced behind him to ensure nothing had snuck up on the two men. When he turned back, he looked on in awe at the display before him.

He had missed the initiation of the attack, but some new force—not an illusion, Victor's flashlight was pointed up now at what was clearly a man—was falling down into the jaws of the T-Rex. It was difficult to see from so far below, and with the monster's body shifting in and out of his line of sight, but the man appeared to be in some state of control over his descent. His right leg was outstretched and pointed down, with his other leg and arms bent, as though they were rudders manipulating his projectile-like shape through the warm air.

The stranger crashed down into the horror's mouth, momentarily choking out the gurgling. The sudden silence following that chilling howl was quickly replaced, though. The beast abruptly *popped*, the shadowy material of its skin and the glowing purple haze buried within vanished, replaced by an equal volume of dust. The dissolving particles started to vanish, twinkling slightly against the beam of the policemen's flashlights and the surrounding violet shimmering of the ground.

As the flakes left the air fully, they revealed in their wake the mysterious man.

"Yeah! Take that you prehistoric *gallina*!" he shouted with pride.

The man—or rather, the boy—was apparently even younger than Officer Levin. Perhaps in his early twenties, if that. As their flashlights now illuminated the scene, no longer stunted by the tyrannosaur, Wallace could see that his legs were somewhat reflective. Not like skin or cloth. They were metal. Robotic.

"Who the Hell are you?" Victor asked with a tone indiscernible as curiosity or attitude.

The young cyborg bent his legs and arms, holding himself for a moment in some sort of heroic pose. "They call me Kicks." he said, his stoic voice betrayed by his childish grin.

"What's your real name, kid." Colton asked, unimpressed. "We don't do superheroes, here."

The boy returned to a normal stature now, pouting slightly with his retort. "That *is* what they call me, it's a nickname!"

"Fine, sure, whatever. What are you doing out here? What's with the—"

"These sweet kicks?!" he interjected, before folding his hands behind his back in shame. "Sorry, I just think it's funny they call me Kicks and now I've got... Anyway, I work for the air force, my dudes. They gave me these 'cause me legs were broke, and recruited me for their secret project."

"Even if I did believe that," Levin started. "That still doesn't explain why you're here, *kid.*"

"Watch it, beat cop." Kicks shot back. "These *monstruos* started attacking us, so they sent me out here to fight them off."

"Alone?"

"Yeah alone, you got a problem with that? I just took down a goddamn *T-Rex* while you *perdedores* were crying for mommy." He glanced back before continuing. "You don't know where you are, huh?"

"No, we were with a team hunting some fleeing suspects out here when we were attacked by these, and just started running." Wallace replied.

"You're about a mile-and-a-half from Area 51, *amigo.*"

"Wait, what?" Victor shouted, drawing the attention of a nearby alligator-shape. "Shouldn't this whole place be fenced off?"

Kicks was paying attention, but started calmly walking over between the approaching monster and the policemen. "It is, moron. How did you think you got in?"

"We followed a train." Colton answered. Kicks lifted up his right leg again, effortlessly holding it above his head in front of him. As the collection of lights started to snap its jaw mere feet away from the boy, he dropkicked the horror's snout, banishing it with a puff of smoke, like the dinosaur before.

"There's no trains here, try again."

"There is now." Victor said, clearly getting annoyed with the boy. "The zombies built it in secret."

Kicks turned around sharply at this. "What did you say?"

"Yeah, that's right. Zombies are real. And they're—"

"No, shut up, I know. They're here?" Kicks asked, clearly agitated.

"Yes, they took a train inside the fence, apparently. Which means they're probably heading for Area 51." Wallace spoke now, having grown tired of the useless banter his young subordinate was contributing.

"But they can't do this; they never made these things before."

"That's a different story. I believe these monsters are being created by a wanted woman called Lady Harrow."

"Wait, what?" It was Kick's turn to be confused.

"You know her?"

"Yeah, man. I used to work with her before the Del Toros went whack. She saved me when I broke my legs."

"Wonderful. So the government's working with criminals now?" Victor interjected. Wallace held up a hand as indication to cut it out.

"No, no, she can't do *this*, man. You're crazy."

"I've seen it, though not on this scale. And I'm sure she's who's really behind the supposed zombies, too."

"Whatever, dude. You're wrong." Kicks said, turning around. "But if those undead freaks are going to Area 51, that's where we gotta go, too."

"We?" Victor asked, ignoring Wallace's direction.

"Yeah, we're under attack. I'm good, but not *that* good. Besides, I'm gonna show you you're wrong about Harrow."

With that, Kicks turned to lead the way back to the military site. His cyborg legs were more than enough to help the three men mow through the nightmares directly in their path, and with each monster he slew, more of the desert was revealed from under the blanket of glowing darkness. And yet the further they travelled, the more prominent the illusionist's supposed influence became.

Wallace didn't know what they were going to find at Groom Lake. But he was going to find out, and if able, he was going to put a stop to it. Be it illusions created by Lady Harrow, zombies back from the dead to steal machine parts, or some wicked combination of the two, he would find the answers to this unique situation. All his problems ended tonight.

Issue 15
Deep as Hell

The railroad tracks had clearly passed through the outer perimeter of the military installation—which was a mystery in and of itself—for R'Bec now stood at what must have been a secondary fence, only perhaps a mile from the base at Groom Lake.

The lights on the horizon were much brighter now. She was almost at her destination.

There were no lights here, though. This barrier was somewhat less secure than what she knew to be at the main exterior fencing, so there was no need for visibility except at the gates. There was still plenty of barbed wiring, of course, and signage indicating the fence was electrically fortified.

Unfortunately for it, and perhaps for R'Bec, her nightmares didn't care.

Snaking through the diamond holes of the wiry metal and growing like disgusting masses of puss and slime, her illusions ripped the obstacle open against her will. The electricity running through the charged caging buzzed and cracked on contact with the dark masses, but did nothing to halt their pulsating purple glow, nor their continued assault of the ineffective wall. It bent inward against the imaginary pressure, granting the alien further passage onto the clandestine soil.

Such a display of her dark power was far from necessary though. A few feet away, the means by which her targets had entered was also clear. The zombies must have simply pressed against the fencing, unfazed by the shocks against their dead and decayed flesh. They pushed down a portion of the fence, barging through and bending the sides of the adjacent portions of the metal in their impatience. Some skin, torn by the loose ends of the wiring, still hung on the edges of their new entrance.

She proceeded, treading carefully on the hellscape that grew beneath her feet. With every step she took, her nightmares filled the gap between the earth and her feet with illusions. Her mind was not playing tricks on her, it was tormenting her. The shadowy, scaly, fuzzy material that glowed and faded with—and yet also somehow, opposite—her heartbeat invaded upon every free inch of the desert around her. It strung itself up between bushes and cacti, burrowed down into snake holes only to grow back out like grotesque orchids. And now they draped themselves like cloth over the fence.

The longer R'Bec was without defense from the long-abandoned thoughts, the more powerful they became, and the further ahead of her they spread. Even behind her she could hear the all-too familiar cries of the monsters she had hated and feared as a child, cannibalizing themselves just to show her what it looked like. What it felt like.

Decades of her bad dreams that had been locked away were now free, and they were more horrifying than ever. As she continued her solemn trek towards Groom Lake, new shapes began to emerge from her subconscious. Faces pressed out from within the variable form of those illusions that caked the ground, screaming at her, spitting and howling and biting. R'Bec stepped with more care, but her slowed pace only gave the horrors better opportunity to sprout up right beneath her feet, ready to gnaw at her ankles for fun and cruelty.

So instead she ran. As fast as she could, she ran. She could never escape her nightmares. But she hoped, maybe, if she could trick herself, that she might outrun them; find herself just a bit ahead of the meaty false floor, be able to just leap out of the jaws of an illusory gargoyle. And even if she couldn't, she had to try. She was willing to try anything, knowing that in the end, there was only one solution—and it was currently unavailable.

The illusions never let up. The faces merged into some horrific conglomeration of shouting heads, like some huge tidal wave of agony and hatred. It washed over the dark desert earth, threatening to swallow R'Bec like the little girl she found herself becoming once again. She tucked her arms close to her chest, trembling even in the warm night air. She closed her eyes to fight back tears, aiming only with her heart to run away from her mind. Stringy, finger-like vines stretched at either side of her, pulling the mass of flickering purple faces along just behind her. Always merely two arm lengths away.

Finally, her feet felt something other than the wet thorns of her nightmares hitting up against them. But this feeling wasn't that of sand or gravel, either. It was concrete.

She opened her eyes; still letting her legs carry her as fast as they could; still holding her arms so close to herself that they might have fused to her sides were it possible.

She had arrived. Area 51.

The soldiers stationed at the base were numerous. Armed guards fought together in teams of two, three, five; all heavily armed, expertly trained, and highly dangerous. All proud and loyal members of their country's military and of their species.

The gunfire was loud and plentiful. It shattered the stillness of the warm desert air like glass. R'Bec found her hands parting from her stomach and rising up to her ears, defending her from the barrage of bullets whizzing through the air all around her. The airmen were fighting with dignity and urgency, like it was the last night of their lives. For many, it would be—they were greatly outnumbered and outmatched.

The zombies were here.

Where the soldiers worked in small groups—clearly having been trained in cooperative combat alongside each other in dedicated teams—their undead opponents swarmed them in huge swathes. For every squad of five guards, there were a dozen horrors surrounding them, leaping over each other and clawing past obstacles and corpses—both animated and not—to reach for the living. Blood splattered the concrete paths and walls of the installation, reflecting back the shining explosions of every rifle shot. The battlefield was illuminated by fire and blood.

And now it was illuminated by R'Bec. Her illusions never seemed to leave any lasting injury for her. They never threatened to kill her, only to break bones or scar flesh—and they had done. But other people were fair game for her subconscious mind. Their physical torture and maiming served as further torment and mental collapse for the mind the nightmares sprouted from, and they were more than eager to seize such opportunities.

Having stopped at the edge of the warzone, R'Bec no longer stood ahead of her nightmares. They caught up to and surrounded her, endeavoring to give the Telignen a perfect view of every horrible act they issued upon both the humans and the zombies.

Now the monsters came in.

From the imaginary black and purple surface beneath her feet erupted a herd of horrific creatures, fanning out from before her and across the base. A monstrous cobra slithered out of the shadows, surrounding a pair of soldiers crouched around their fallen comrades, threatening to swallow them whole. A flock of crows burst from the now-shadow-slathered wall, cawing a hollow, never-ending screech that forced many of the guards to drop their weapons and hold their ears, as the glowing purple beaks pecked at and dissected the stringy flesh of the zombies.

Six or seven members of already dismembered teams found themselves in a silent truce with a gathering of their undead attackers, momentarily working together against the nightmarish threat. But even that uneasy alliance found itself defeated; crushed under the pulsating foot of a huge spinosaurus whose head reached just under the apex of the surrounding hangars.

The scene was madness. R'Bec felt as though she could do nothing but watch helplessly as the horrors crawling from the recesses of her mind tore apart the assembled humans, both alive and dead. And the illusions knew that. Even as the meaningless faces once again pressed up from against the furrowed pulsating ground to butt and gnaw at her feet and legs, she found herself unable—or unwilling—to move.

Then a light shone in her mind. Something inside of her reached out and touched her alien soul. Not a purple glimmer, like her nightmares. A brilliant blue energy; a beautiful one.

"Keep going, H." R'Bec found her lips mouthing words that were not her own. She couldn't hear herself over the mumbled roars and murmuring wails of her nightmares and their victims, but she felt the wind passing through her throat before it became stifled by the rest of the cruel world. "You didn't come all this way to not be a hero."

"I don't know what I'm doing. I can't think straight. They won't let me." she spoke back to herself—to the voice inside of her that was using her mouth.

"They *are* you." Again, her own voice spoke to her, but they weren't her words. She choked slightly on the coarse air, before it continued through her. "Don't you see, H? The globe wasn't anything special. It was a crutch. You can fight your nightmares all on your own. Didn't your parents tell you as much?"

Her parents.

R'Bec's mind trailed back to that day. She hadn't left home yet; she was only a little girl. She didn't yet know what she was.

"I can't sleep, mommy. They hurt me, it hurts! Make it stop."

Her mother looked to one of her fathers. R'Bec couldn't see it then, but her face was one of knowing regret.

"It's okay, my child. They're all in your imagination, and only you can make them go away."

"That's right, sweetheart." her other father spoke up. "It's going to be hard, but I know you can do it. Whatever you have to do to make them think you're stronger than them. Because you are. Give them funny names, pretend you have a sword and a shield—show 'em who's boss!"

R'Bec took her face out from her mother's folded elbow. She sniffed, and her father wiped away her tears. She hugged him, and then the other.

"Now go back to bed, little one. Go back to dreaming of the stars where you belong. Tuck your nightmares away."

As R'Bec returned to her bedroom, she again saw a look on her three parents' faces that at the time she couldn't understand. But in her memories, she knew it was one of fear and sympathy. They knew what was wrong. And they knew that they were wrong.

The funny names did not help much. Mister Snuggles still sat on her chest, weighing on her lungs. Squeaky McFarts nibbled at her toes as always. She was at least able to scare away the worst one with her sword: Fuzzywuzzymuffin. But still her nightmares tormented her. Every single night. For years and years, they formed her into the tough little girl that took shit from nobody—no bullies, no stupid adults—but who was afraid to go into the dark alone, for fear she might fall asleep. For fear her nightmares would get her, and hurt her.

"It never worked. I couldn't do it without the globe." R'Bec said to the voice inside her, pulling her back into reality; back onto the fateful battlefield.

"You didn't understand it then. Now you do. Only you can fight your nightmares and face your demons. You have everything you need, H."

With those final words, the light inside her vanished. R'Bec was once again alone against the dark.

"Thank you, Jenna." she said to no one.

With clenched fists, R'Bec marched slowly across the dark slime covering the concrete ground. Some of the nearby monsters seemed to hesitate on recognizing her motion, but they remained focused on their current tasks. There were still plenty of humans and zombies around, and so the nightmares hadn't started attacking each other yet, and only paid mild attention to her.

There was no need for theatrics. No need for fancy weapons or attention to detail. These were nightmares; illusions created by her own subconscious mind, invincible to conventional means. The military tools and tactics of Area 51—and even the swarming strength of the mysterious undead—were no match for them. Only R'Bec could stand against them. She had to fight fire with fire.

She conjured a simple ball in her hand, perhaps six inches in diameter. She didn't need to throw it; instead she willed it to float before her, then sent it flying toward the spinosaurus illusion that stood a few dozen yards ahead of her. As it did, it expanded, and R'Bec summoned magnificent golden flames all around it, consuming the imaginary sphere and exploding as it neared its target.

Her aim was true. It ought to be, she had imagined it so. The great ball reached the dinosaur and ignited its scaly black hide. All of the purple lights beneath that dark skin glowed as it reared its head in terror. In just a few moments, the monster dissolved into black dust.

But R'Bec wasn't done yet. Now with the nightmare burst, she was back in control of its elements. The illusory dust it had become remained, rather than dissipating into the air as usual. Each individual flake fluttered there, until she willed for those too to ignite in glorious blaze. They expanded outward, falling back to the earth to burn down every nightmare they might land upon.

The cobra sank its fangs into the ground and wriggled its powerful body, violently trying to shake away the fire that had caught on its tail. But the streams were unrelenting, and trailed up to its head, burning away at the black flesh and violet lights shining within. Finally, with a hiss of pain, the serpent's body went limp before collapsing into itself. Into dust.

The crows continued to fly as more and more of their flock succumbed to the inferno. The sky—though still dark—burnt red and orange as the hundreds of oversized illusory birds changed from brilliant magenta to striking gold. As one finally relented and burst into ash, that ash ignited for more of its kin to fly through, further toasting themselves and the illusions below.

The soldiers took the hint. The tides were turning. No longer hampered by the nightmares, they turned their muzzles back to their initial foes: the zombie hordes.

The horrors returned to their droning swarms, surrounding the Area 51 guards as they had before. R'Bec had to keep her focus on the fire—it was too sophisticated to maintain as a second nature with the level of efficacy her nightmares demanded—but she was still able to provide some minor aid to the humans.

She created intentional illusions of plaster and ooze intended to look like and blend in with those fantasies that were outside of her control, and sicced them on the armies of the undead. Her new purple-glowing creatures crawled up under their feet and upturned their lifeless bodies, swallowing them in the bright darkness and ripping them apart so thoroughly that the strange stringy material inside could not possibly reassemble them.

At this display, the soldiers began to retreat, meeting up with their associates and aiding in reclaiming the base from the corpses. With each area freed of undead control, R'Bec burnt the remaining illusions there, destroying the nightmares still attempting to close in.

R'Bec was far from through, though. She wasn't cured, she merely had a new coping mechanism. Her nightmares continued to generate outside the fog of their charred and dissolving kin. Even beneath her feet, where she was unable to safely set fire to the horrors attacking her, they remained vicious as ever.

She kept moving. As new nightmares came into view, she created new golden torches to incinerate them. As a squad of humans was about to fall prey to a zombie horde, she allowed her imagination to lash out and annihilate them. Yet still, always, the ghouls regrouped. What few she was able to completely decommission was not enough to seriously dent their numbers. She could barely decimate the undead menace.

But she could not fall victim to these thoughts. They only strengthened those dark portions of her mind vying to reclaim control of her spirit. R'Bec kept moving.

As much as she wanted to ensure the humans would be safe, she knew that as long as she remained here, they would be forever in danger, if only from her. And their safety was not what drew her here. The creatures were here for something. This attack was calculated and full-scale. Not an invasion, but a cleverly disguised heist. She had to find what they were after and stop them. Then she could worry about suppressing her nightmares.

R'Bec spotted a group of zombies entering a hangar door. No, more than a group. The whole army was slowly and secretly making its way there, sneaking into the interior of the complex.

As the last of a small group made it through, she swiftly came up behind them. Remembering her difficulty with dispatching them at the Cosmopolitan, and even still here at Groom Lake with overextended illusions, R'Bec opted for the stealthy approach. She quietly followed the entourage inside the hanger, before they started descending down some stairs and deeper into the installation.

The air was colder here, and the lights were dimmed. Likely due to the present attack. Whatever the case, the zombies seemed to be responding to the new environment. They were somewhat less feral, here.

No. That wasn't right. The air and lighting had nothing to do with it. It was cold in the Cosmopolitan, and they were always in the dark. They were behaving differently because they were unobserved—or believed they were.

They walked upright now, and slowly. More casually, with little sense of urgency.

But it didn't stay that way. As R'Bec moved away from the inferno above, her nightmares began to catch up. They weren't following her; they didn't need to. They simply generated all around her again, and even ahead of her.

The horrors ahead of her returned to their agitated state as a great boar—Mister Snuggles; larger than when she was a child, but smaller than it would be out in the wastes—barreled through the hall and straight through their party.

A number of the creatures were impaled on the nightmare's tusks, and some found themselves trampled by its squishy but powerful hooves. Most were merely pressed against the concrete walls of the corridor, though. However, none of them were injured enough to be incapacitated. Rather than continue its tirade straight for R'Bec, who was still concealed from the zombies, Snuggles chose to turn around like some horrific, slimy ragdoll. It charged once again at the swarm.

The creatures readied themselves. Two zombies on either side grabbed hold of the outstretched arms of their skewered relatives. They sharply pulled downward on their arms; the sinews holding their decaying bodies together became visible, but held tight at the teamwork up-to-now undocumented from the undead.

At the disturbance, Mister Snuggles' porcine head bucked up, snapping its imaginary neck with a sound that made R'Bec cringe with every muscle at once.

She peered around the corner again. The nightmarish boar was dissolving, but the zombies lay huddled on the ground, too; defeated and deceased once again.

Confused, R'Bec entered the hallway fully to investigate. She knelt down over one of the corpses.

Previously, the eyes of the undead creatures were black pools of nothingness. No light reflected upon them, but there was clear shape inside their sockets. Now, though, this body's eyes were properly empty. She could see the inside of its skull—dark, but not impossibly black like before.

She summoned an imaginary knife and gently peeled away at the skin on the creature's wrist. It parted easily for her, and revealed... nothing. The muscles were totally rotted away, and its bones rattled loose inside the fleshy bag. No black strings held it together.

R'Bec examined the cadaver's head. Something was lying on the ground beside it, a small thread. It ended abruptly only two or three feet away, but she traced it back to the nape of the dead human's neck. It had previously extended—and expanded—inside the corpse, animating it.

When Mister Snuggles' head was forcefully reared, its tusks had severed the line between all of these zombies and... whatever master pulled at their strings.

These weren't zombies. They were puppets. Human bodies made to dance and fight on near-invisible threads. This was more serious than she had previously imagined. This wasn't some epidemic, it was an act of cruelty. A crime against nature. Someone was using the dead like a mask for their own ends. R'Bec would not stand for it.

But she couldn't linger here. Her nightmares were reforming again. The slimy faces crept up on her now, caking the walls. She hurriedly continued through the corridor, looking back in horror as the pulsating shadow consumed the dead humans lying helpless on the floor. But she could do nothing about it. She couldn't risk setting fires in here—although she called them illusions, these extensions of her mind were very real if she gave them enough focus to be. And the focus necessary to kill her nightmares was great; she would risk choking herself, or worse.

So she went on her way. She forgot about the bodies behind her, for now. And her nightmares proceeded right alongside her.

R'Bec walked with purpose now. She didn't care when the faces pressed up from the floor, opening their mouths wide for her foot to step into. She didn't care when arms stretched out from the walls to poke and grope and violently pinch at her. And as much as she wanted to—as much as it hurt not to—she didn't care when she stumbled upon a group of undead slaves, and was forced to watch her nightmares maim and slaughter them with even more cruelty than before, knowing her pain in viewing such a display. She just couldn't care.

She needed to be dispassionate now. She needed to be fueled by purpose, by what was right. But sometimes, it can be hard to separate logic from rage. Righteousness from hurt. She found her memories wandering back again.

She was back in her home, with her parents again. She knew the day well. The smells in the house, the angle of the shadows denoting an afternoon sun. This was the day R'Bec left home.

She was seventeen. She'd spent nearly a decade being tortured every night by nightmarish creatures intent on hurting her. She wept every day in fear of her bed, knowing that her mother and fathers could not help her.

"R'Bec," one of her fathers called to her. "Come here, we need to talk to you about something."

She came obediently, although distant as always. She had dyed her hair red, and she wore black clothes and lipstick. Small acts of rebellion. She didn't hate her parents—not yet. But she resented their ineptitude for her experiences.

"Sit down, we need to have a family discussion."

"Sure, fine." she said without conviction.

"This is going to be a lot to take in, sweetheart." her mother began. "But please hear us out. We love you, okay?"

"Your nightmares are real, R'Bec." her other father said, without missing a beat. "They're not all in your head. But they do come from your head. You have the power to create whatever you imagine, we all do."

"We're a species called Telignen. We're aliens, all four of us, from the planet Peplorix." Her first father specified. To prove their first point, he raised his palm and created, hovering there, an illusion of the planet. It was like a marble; red fields surrounded by blue seas, all decorated with gold mountains under purple clouds.

"We brought you here to protect you. Peplorix wasn't safe anymore, and we wanted you to grow up happy." her mother added.

"But you're sick, R'Bec. That's why your nightmares hurt you. You can't control your power, and..." her other father continued. "And we can't help you. None of us are doctors, and Earth doctors don't know what you are, much less what to do for you."

"But we're going to keep you safe, sweetheart." her first father reassured her, sitting down beside her. "We're going to be with you every step of the way, from now on. We may not be able to stop your nightmares, but we can help you live with them. We will. Because we love you."

R'Bec didn't know what to say in that moment. Every sentence her parents added on each other felt like a stab in the lungs. She couldn't breathe. Her arms clutched her aching stomach. Her ears burned, and her eyes stung with the harsh air against her welling tears. She couldn't speak.

She just stood up and ran to her room. She locked the door, knowing it didn't make a difference. She just lay on her bed and cried.

They had lied to her. All of those years, they refused to tell her the truth. It would have been one thing if they waited until she started having her nightmares. But they kept her in the dark even after that, for almost ten years. She was an alien. She felt alone in the world already, fending for herself against the terrors she experienced every night. It had torn her apart in the day, and as her nightmares crept into the corners of her vision even in her waking hours, she thought she was going mad. She had become so distant from everyone, pushed people away. Friends and crushes and mentors fell to the side as she lost her grip on reality, completely alone. And now to find out that she wasn't even human. It broke her heart and stomped on the pieces of her already crumbling mind.

And it was her parents' fault. They brought her here, to live on this miserable rock. They didn't plan for her to be sick. They couldn't handle her nightmares, so then they lied to her and only made things worse. It was all their fault.

A nightmarish hand gripping her throat pulled R'Bec back into the present, back into reality. She was in the underground complexes of Area 51 again, moving through her waking dreams and the enslaved corpses, seeking her true enemy. Whether she was wrong back then or not didn't matter now. She was more than a sick little girl. She was even more than a Telignen. She was her own person. She was a hero.

This would be her ultimate test of everything she had accomplished up to now. She overcame her nightmares once, and she would do it again without her lucky charm. She had faced villains and criminals and undead horrors, and tonight, it would all end. R'Bec followed the threads drifting through the corridors, past hangars and labs and prison cells and barracks.

Eventually she would need to dispel her nightmares, for the safety of those around her. But for tonight, R'Bec would endure their torment, because if there was one thing she could count on, it was that whatever puppeteer stood at the end of these ropes would have to fight them, too.

Issue 16
No Kind Words

"Ya see? That proves it!"

Detective Wallace, Officer Levin, and the apparent hero, Kicks, had been moving through the desert at a slow pace. Kicks dispatched each dreaded illusion with ease, but the two policemen couldn't move as fast as his supplemental legs. They walked slowly, recollecting their strength and breath from their earlier sprint.

The trio now stood at what was, at one point, an electric fence. It was effectively defunct now, though. Two gaping holes had rendered the wiry metal irrelevant.

One looked like it had simply been pushed down, wildly and ignorantly pressed upon until it no longer barred the path. Whatever force caused the intrusion also bent the edges of the barrier on either side of the toppled section.

The other looked as though the metal was simply ripped apart. Like something had woven between the diamond mesh and expanded, again without interest in or notice of the electricity running through it. This scenario was made even more likely by the remnants of the force which had obviously caused it: slimy black masses that glowed with an uneasy violet aura, slathered all along the ground and coated across the top and broken edges of the enclosure.

The young Latino was grinning like an idiot, his eyes wide and expectant in Wallace's face, and his finger outstretched, pointing at the two adjacent breaches.

"Okay, I give. What does this prove?" Victor said, shrugging. Wallace's eye flinched at the Officer's annoying tone, but he agreed—there was nothing interesting about the scene.

"Are you sure you're cops?" Kicks replied, returning his extended arm to meet his other at his hips, posing in frustrating and exasperation. "There's two holes here: one for the zombies and one for the monsters. Ignoring that Lady Harrow can't do either, this proves that she couldn't be behind both, or there'd only be one hole."

"This material that the monsters appear to be made of could have produced the second hole without thinking about it." Colton replied. "It's clearly moving on its own."

"More proof that it's separate from the zombies! Man, come on!"

"It really isn't, kid." Victor said, easing his aggression some.

"That's *Kicks*. Now let me walk you *idiotas* through it. If Lady Harrow is making both of these like you somehow think, that means she would have to be in control of them. You said illusions, right? She would have to be paying attention to what they're doing, manipulating them. So the illusions wouldn't have broken the gate by accident, so she's not behind them.

"So, if she were controlling the zombies—which would be stupid and wrong, but I'll humor you—then how do you explain this?"

The young man had walked over to the edge of the fence that had been bent around the edges of the first hole. The wiring was snapped and torn in several places. As the section was disconnected from the rest of the fence, standing between that hole and the one the shadowy puss had created, it was not electrified. He safely gripped a small piece of evidence between his fingers, plucking it from the metal.

Colton shone his flashlight on the flake. It was a piece of skin. Grey and dead, but unmistakable.

"Harrow's illusions broke when she left the scene before, Colt." Levin said.

Victor was right. And so was Kicks.

The zombies were real. The monsters were real. Lady Harrow had nothing to do with either.

His world shattered. Everything he knew broke apart like a window, fracturing his understanding of reality. Then, new information flooded in—new realizations. They reached into the cracks of his ideals and dreams. His brain swelled with understanding as the knowledge settled, aligning itself with what he already held true. His worldview had been expanded. It was scary, and infuriating. Then it was calm.

"We have to get to the base."

"No apology, really? No 'I'm sorry—'"

"Quiet." Wallace interrupted. "I was wrong. That doesn't mean we get to stand around and cry or laugh about it. Area 51 is in trouble. The zombies are after something there, and since they already have the marconium, the world could be in danger. And these things... they're getting stronger by the minute, and wider, too. Kicks, you're the only one who can handle them, so for God's sake will you take the win on your own time and help us deal with this crisis?"

The boy gulped. "Sorry. Let's go; it's not much further." he said, shaking his head and again taking the lead. They opted for the hole that had been pushed in, recognizing it had fewer of the unsightly masses running through and around it.

Although, much of the desert was still caked with the stuff. And even more once they passed through the final perimeter. Wallace could see the lights on the horizon, directly in line with where Kicks was guiding them. Naturally, the horrific creatures swarmed between the unlikely group and their destination, concealing the glow from time to time with their own dark glimmering bodies. But, as the cyborg plowed through a pack of cackling hyenas, the Detective thought he caught a brilliant flash of gold replace the barely-piercing white light emanating from the base at Groom Lake.

The ground came hurtling towards him like a tidal wave of dirt and concrete. From his perspective, anyway. In fact, it was Kicks who was falling back to Earth from some fifty feet in the sky. He angled himself accordingly, moving with precision and grace, slicing the dry air with his outstretched leg. This was only his second time testing his airtime with the prosthetics, but his skill was showing already. He crashed down on his target with ease: a twenty-foot kangaroo-shaped atrocity, whose purple glow and shadowy skin shattered into empty dust upon his impact with the center of its flat head.

He spiraled through the fluttering remains of the monster as they vanished, slowing and controlling his descent before his metal feet tapped the ground with the faintest ring, as though he had been gently set down by a caring hand.

These mechanical replacements for his broken legs were new technology—cutting edge. Before now, the efficiency of commercial prosthetic legs had always been hampered by one factor above all else: weight. They had to be light enough for the motors to be able to move the frame. That required not only lightweight materials, but also small or awkward power supplies, which created their own problems. Marconium power changed all that.

With just two marconium batteries—one for each leg—Snow Dynamics Enterprises developed a prosthetic system that looked and felt sleek, with improved mobility, and of course, lifespan. In fact, the company devoted an entire department to the research and development of commercial prosthetics, all reliant on built-in marconium batteries, if not the many energy storage and usage technologies that came about because of it.

Of course, the standard Snow Dynamics products didn't have the strength to kick a person fifty feet into the air, or smash through bulletproof monsters. They were for civilian use, after all, and the company was wholly against any kind of weapons-grade invention, and limited this research ruthlessly.

However, once the team at Groom Lake had acquired a pair of marconium-powered legs, there was little Marco Nieve could do to stop them from modifying it how they wished. The resistors limiting the battery's supply were removed, and the motors were replaced with industrial strength machinery. The casing was armored and grafted with additional conveniences, or at least the capacity to add them as they were developed. All they needed was a volunteer.

Enter Kicks. A youthful, eager young man with legs rendered useless by a supervillain. His heroic aspirations made him the perfect candidate for the project. It wasn't without heroic intentions, of course. But the moral ambiguity was something that needed to be kept within the confines of the base, and so someone who understood the blurry grey line already was ideal.

The two policemen didn't need to know all those details, though. They would do their job better without, anyway.

Once the trio had arrived at the collection of hangars and offices making up the occupied space of Area 51, it was clear to them what each needed to do with the scene, and they silently agreed to part ways and handle the threat.

Wallace and Levin joined with a squad of soldiers engaged in a skirmish with a crowd of hungry ghouls. Small fires were scattered about, making both mobility and visibility difficult, but the extra hands would help to even the odds some. Their aim was not to subdue the undead, but largely to evacuate the area. This was a battle they could not win, and that became obvious by what Kicks was expected to handle.

Someone clearly had the bright idea to try and burn the monsters that attacked the base at Groom Lake. And perhaps it even worked some, too—there were still some golden embers flittering in the air, carried by the breeze created by the warm air of the still lingering fires. But they let up even less than the zombies. The horrors simply grew back in greater numbers and greater forms. Perhaps this was in outrage from the blazing attack, but something told Kicks that the nightmarish creatures were only becoming more powerful because whatever was drawing the strange substance which made up their bodies was now here. A glance in the distance seemed to confirm that indeed, while they still maintained control of the territory outside the main base, their numbers had dwindled staggeringly. Like the ghouls, this was intended to be the monsters' last stand.

The Detective and Officer had separated some, apparently to guide two disparate groups closer to one another. Both of their enemies had strength in numbers, but they could make use of that natural law, too.

The zombies were tough, and the most immediate threat to the soldiers, but Kicks had to focus on the beasts. Although they slaughtered both alive and undead men and women, they did so in larger sweeps. And where the ghouls were hard to kill, only Kicks could banish the horrors.

And so he leapt once again; not upwards this time, but forwards. He made the motions as though he was running, but his strides were so great that he took only two steps to travel some twenty-five feet. His eyes were trained on an enormous anteater. As its tongue slipped out from its unusual snout, threatening to reach around and slurp up Victor's assembled squad, Kicks took one final step—one with great upward force.

His right leg was his strongest in the past, but now they were evenly matched. Still, the right side of his body remained the dominant in all other aspects, and so he had better control when he kicked off and landed with that leg. He therefore angled his left leg like a rudder, helping him to drag his torso back and become a projectile, angling the right appendage back ahead of him, leading him to his mark.

Impact.

It wasn't a perfect shot—something must have caught in his eye for a moment—but he still smashed squarely into the anteater's eye. He broke through, and quickly swung his left leg back and around, letting him turn his body to face the concrete below.

Once his pronged feet—designed for better mobility and shock absorbency, rather than imitation of their organic predecessors—met a barrier, he knew he'd met the wall of the building previously behind the monster. It was tough to gauge his distance from the ground, as the ashy remains of his victim hadn't totally dissolved yet, but he kicked off anyway, letting himself fall downward for his arms to catch him in a roll.

It was a... less than graceful landing. But he was uninjured. He stood up quickly, hoping his blunder had been concealed. Whether it had or hadn't, the others didn't seem to care. He quickly walked over to the team Levin was with, which united with Wallace's own squad after pressing through a few more zombies; only two were dispatched, but the others were pushed back some and held there by a new creature's beginning materialization.

"That's all the monsters, boss, but not for long. They just keep coming." Kicks informed the Detective.

"I can see that. It looks like they're focusing their numbers and strength here. But even still... This doesn't feel full."

"Things went from bad to worse after that Indian woman got here, but they've stagnated now." One of the soldiers offered, kicking away the face of a clawing zombie from under the swirly dark mass of purple lights slowly forming between them.

"What? Native American, red hair, crazy powers?" Levin asked excitedly.

"That's her. They started attacking with more force when she showed up, but then she pulled that fire out of nowhere and burnt 'em down. They've been regrouping since, but I think they're getting weaker. Or maybe stronger, but at a slower rate."

"Where is she, now?" Wallace demanded. Kicks saw the Detective glance at him, as though considering whether it was worth saying 'I told you so.'

"I think I saw her chasing after a group of these things, into one of the hangars." Another of the airmen spoke up.

"Which one?!" Kicks and Colton shouted together.

"I don't know!" she replied.

That was no help. Still, Kicks couldn't blame her. She was fighting for her life here. It was dark, and smoky, and not of this world.

"Alright, let's keep moving around the base, we need to find where she went. When we find Lady Harrow, we find answers. Then we can stop this madness." Wallace decreed. The airmen seemed all too eager to follow him, having accepted that their rank meant nothing against the menaces surrounding them. They moved onward, but Kicks stayed still.

"Uh, Detective... I think there's a problem." he said with concern.

"What's tha—oh." Colton replied, turning around. As he did, his eyes caught Kicks' concern.

The nightmarish material had been taking a while to reform. At the time, the group thought nothing of it—they welcomed the brief moment of respite. But now, Kicks understood why it was taking so long.

It was so huge that even now the new monster's form was finishing its assembly. But the basic shape was unmistakable, even from on the ground, looking up into the dim sky and at the unclear outline of its dark mass and purple glowing innards. They flashed like synapses and pulsed like veins, the light pumping along inside its enormous body. From the talon-clad feet that dug into the ground before them; up through the great muscular legs that curled under its hulking body in casual comfort; extending out

191

from just behind its shoulder blades and through the thinner, fleshy flaps of its wings; inside its towering neck that brought its frilled, reptilian head well over the base's largest hangar—by Kick's estimate, it was only just as high as he could jump at full force, and that was lying on its stomach.

There were still a few of the horrific creatures around, but most of the space—both on the ground and in the sky—was dominated by the great nightmarish dragon.

"Okay, we'll keep going. You handle that thing."

"You say that like you think I can fight it, *amigo*." Kicks said. He was unsure of himself against something so massive.

"So it's big, but it's not any different than any of the others. Still the same flesh and blood; just kick it, Kicks" Levin said, nudging along the airmen to continue their route. The final touches were being put on the dragon's body, and now it was preparing to stand up and attack.

As much as he appreciated the Officer's attempt to encourage him, his new friends didn't realize what exactly went into breaking down these monsters.

The marconium batteries in his legs had a great power output, but he'd rip them off his waist if he used all of it at once. He was doing more when he landed his curled foot against the horrors than just kicking; he was increasing the output of his shock absorbers, deflecting the resisting force and amplifying it, rather than meeting it equally. On paper, it was not unlike the famous Shockdrop suit, but trading shockwaves for impact strength.

But Marco's sidekick's suit had the advantage of sending energy outward, and protecting itself from the frequencies of its attacks. Kicks' legs had to suffer the forces it put out, as they were a result of physical contact. The laws of physics were fickle, and they could cost him the ability to continue fighting if he overextended himself.

The Tyrannosaurus Rex already required nearly the maximum his doctors and scientists estimated he could take without hurting himself or the prosthetics. If the dragon required much more…

But he had to try. Solving this mess required Wallace and the soldiers to find Lady Harrow—or whoever they think they saw—and right now, they were easy prey for the unreasonably large lizard.

Kicks leapt into the air as per normal, taking advantage of the extra space provided by the clearing of those undead that had been nearby to get in some extra initial momentum.

The dragon was tall. His estimates had been a little short—when he reached the height of his arc, he was still a few feet shy of the monster's snout, which seemed to curl its sloppy, ill-formed lips in a delighted sneer. But Kicks wasn't aiming for the head.

As he began to descend, he once again extended his right leg, using his left and both arms as rudders to propel him through the air. He was still falling incredibly fast, but he had some limited control of his trajectory. He positioned himself to land right between the horror's wings, at the point its back met its neck. Physiology hadn't been relevant for defeating the nightmares up to now, but since he couldn't risk using his full strength, he needed to think a little smarter.

He started at a power level closer to what he used on the kangaroo. It had been smaller than the T-Rex, but hopefully the weaker portion of the slimy scaled body would crumble to that degree just as easily as that previous creature's head.

He didn't know what to expect. He didn't prepare any kind of follow through—he had no basis with which to judge how to brace himself. When he had defeated each of the preceding horrors, they collapsed on impact, and he passed through their dust without effort. When the bowed metal that made up his foot met the glowing shade of the dragon, though, he nearly fell over. All his weight on one leg offset his balance in a way Kicks wasn't prepared for.

His right leg bent at the artificial knee, the shock absorbers doing their part by instinctively letting him crouch down. He found himself kneeling on the back of the huge dragon, the rims of his metallic thighs vaguely rubbing the skin of his hips.

As the dragon's neck turned to allow its face to peer down between its wings, Kicks saw once again—from below, in horrifyingly indefinite distance and shadow—the eyes of his monstrous opponent. It didn't look particularly bothered. Its snarl was not one of frustration, but nor was it one of bemusement. It was more... mild curiosity, perhaps?

Maybe he had hurt it some, but not enough to collapse it.

"Yeah! You like that, you giant lazy bastard?" he taunted.

Its response was nonverbal, but the sudden lunge of its frilled head downward—making use of the exceptional flexibility of its neck to attempt to drive its own horns down into its back, and straight through its attacker—could probably be interpreted as "Get the Hell off me, stupid human." That's how Kicks chose to read that cue, anyway.

He kicked the heel of his foot into the skin of the beast, digging what little he could into the unrelenting shadowy mass of blinking violet nodes to get even a little traction. He pushed off from there, propelling himself backwards along the spine of the creature. The slimy, but still sharp and powerful horn was just able to graze him. He felt only the side of it, thankfully; nothing was pierced or cut. But it was still a heart-dropping experience.

He slid with one foot along the slippery fur of the monster before it once again reared its head in attack. He set his other curved appendage into the dragon's hide once more, kicking off in a different direction: away from the beast and back down to the concrete.

Unfortunately, he had failed to look down beforehand, and found himself only a few feet away from three converging groups of zombies. At first they seemed uninterested in him—they were walking off in the same direction, seemingly in pursuit of the flight of airmen and the two police officers. But Kicks only had a few moments to collect himself before a casual glance back revealed him to the ghouls.

They lunged at him, eager to take what few lives were available now in the chaos of the three-way battle.

Zombies were easy, though. It only took a few kicks to dislodge their head, separating the brain and permanently killing them as expected. But it was a long process, and he could only work on one at a time, for the most part. What didn't help, either, was having a fifty-plus foot dragon also trying to get in on the action. And try it did.

Kicks lifted his leg up to let loose a barrage of swift and successive thrusts at the nearest hobbling corpse. It tried to swipe its head as though it were some loose appendage, using its mouth as an attempted grip. But not only were its reflexes insufficient—

though admittedly lightning-fast—the metal at the end of Kicks' leg would only have eased his objective, breaking into the monster's jaw and destroying the head from the inside.

But he didn't get to do that. Apparently incapable of breathing fire, the huge dragon swiped its head over the crowd of zombies that circled the cyborg, curling its neck around them with horrific grace. It lacked proper eyes, but the collection of magenta lights dancing inside its gelatinous head seemed to stare at him— through him. The force of the creature's quick motion knocked Kicks off-balance, and he returned his right leg to the ground to catch himself.

He turned his attention back to the dragon, recognizing it wouldn't let him focus on the horde without intrusion. Although it snapped at two of the zombies now, Kicks recognized that he was its true enemy. So he would give it what it wanted.

He leapt into the air, consciously keeping his arc at around fifteen feet, as the horror's head was only ten or so at its tallest point: right between the eyes.

Rather than perform his typical projectile-like motion as he had become accustomed to, he opted for a more active approach. He began somersaulting through the air; his arms were bent and held at right angles, and along with his bent left leg, he was able to control his velocity as always, despite the continuous roll. He kept the last metal appendage outstretched—this served not only as his intended weapon, but also to drag and slow his descent.

He kicked the power of his next swing up to that which he had used back in the desert against what was up-to-then the largest of the nightmares he had faced. He was using his old form then, and was less strategic in choosing the point of impact. The new swinging kick style, plus his added attention to the details of where he landed, would hopefully prove to be enough to fell the beast without taking the toll on his body any higher.

"Take this, *pendejo*!" he shouted, completing his final spin.

Impact.

His curved metal foot crashed into the dragon's sticky hide. Not that he felt that, anyway.

The creature's head did dissolve. He fell through and to the ground with ease, as he had done many times that night. His landing was less than ideal, resulting in his legs spread apart on the concrete; one fully ahead of him, one behind. He'd never been able to do the splits with his old thighs!

But it wasn't over. He looked up through the dissipating particles of the monster's head to check his work.

Something was wrong. Whether it was because this creature—the king of all of the horrors if there ever was one—was more powerful than the rest and possessed its own unique abilities, or that it was just so massive and collective that its whole form could not be struck down in a single hit, Kicks couldn't tell. But the dragon's neck remained curled around him. Its fat, pulsating body still hung over one of the hangars. Its wings still filled the night sky with those damned purple blips.

Only its head had been dissolved. And even that began to reform before his eyes. Slowly, like before, the shining darkness began to grow out of the stump at the end of its greater form, not apparently taking from anywhere, but amassing more shape nonetheless. It was a big head, but as whatever force was allowing this to happen didn't need to also generate a whole body, it was beginning to sprout much more quickly than before.

"*Mierda*, no!" Kicks shouted up at the nightmare, knowing full well that if it was listening or could understand, that it didn't care for his pleas.

He acted without thought or hesitation. On instinct alone, he kicked off from the ground. He didn't intend to, but he leapt up with the full force he'd just used.

But even still, he wasn't thinking clearly. He was trying to be fast, desperately striving to pull out a win, at any cost. And so he didn't even consider the need to reposition his body in mid-air to let his robotic legs lead the way. They served only as propulsion for his outstretched arm and balled fist. Kicks was aiming a marconium-powered punch straight for the end of the monster's neck. No new head—or even worse, *heads*—would sprout on his watch.

Impact.

It hurt more than he expected. He didn't really feel anything when he kicked those previous creatures. The slight press of the metal against his hips from his foot meeting their mark, sure. But he hadn't touched the material with his skin before now. It was coarse, but also somehow silky.

The collision also sent shooting pain through his arm and shoulder. Nothing was broken that he could tell, but it was a sensation he hadn't dealt with before now.

Still, he'd accomplished his goal.

Although he fell back to the ground clumsily—not granted the same follow through as when his feet delivered the blow—he looked up in excitement to see that a large chunk of the neck he had just lunged at was now disappeared. Only dust remained in its place, and that too was vanishing with every adrenal beat of his heart.

The dragon once again began to regenerate what was lost from the stem, perhaps seven feet from where its neck met its shoulders.

Again, Kicks sprang up from the ground and toward his opponent.

This time, with newfound understanding and confidence, he gathered the composure to smartly adjust himself into a flying kick position. He aimed not for the growing end of the monster, though, but for its brilliant glowing chest, just visible between the huge forearms stretching down into the base.

He had made sure to propel himself so that when he passed through the fluttering remains of the dragon's remaining neck and front torso, he would maintain momentum and come out near the top of his arc above the monster's hind legs. As expected, the creature dissolved easily in its weakened state. Gravity took the liberty of letting Kicks fall back down, and with his signature projectile form, he crashed into the nightmare one final time. The last of its torso popped into a puff of smoke and dust, and without it, the horror's remaining legs and tail collapsed into nothingness as well. He'd done it.

But it wasn't without cost. Kicks returned to the ground safely—and in a safe portion of the base, as luck would have it; there were no zombies within sight, evidently having returned to wherever they were going before he'd attracted their attention—and examined himself for bruises.

Robot legs didn't bruise, however. They broke. And while he was still able to stand and walk without trouble, very clear damage had been done to his artificial appendages. So many high-powered collisions so quickly had worn them significantly. The shock absorbers were shot, and he could feel tell some interior support was starting to fail, as the edges of the metal grinded a bit more forcefully against the skin of his hips. He would be fine with a little tune-up, but that required engineers.

"Those eggheads better still be alive." he thought aloud. "Oh gosh, the cops!"

With that notion, Kicks ran off in the direction he hoped he had seen Detective Wallace and Officer Levin leading the gathered survivors, and he prayed that they were safe, and close to ending this crisis.

Issue 17
Angel of Hell

She had been wandering the maze of dim halls for some time. The underground complex of Area 51 was more extensive than she could have imagined. Granted, its actual size was likely being exaggerated by her disorienting nightmares.

The horrors of her subconscious would not let up, and R'Bec could tell they were only growing stronger. As her mind numbed to the pain of watching the undead puppets be torn apart by those extensions of herself that were out of her control, she did her best to banish as much of those evils as she could. She was unable to completely dispel them, of course, but with some effort, she was able to focus a majority of the gelatinous shadows up to the surface, far away from her. What remained of the base would be put in danger—it may even prompt Fuzzywuzzymuffin, her most powerful and feared nightmare to emerge—but it would be a greater catastrophe if she didn't stop the force at the end of these strings from claiming its prize.

So she continued, setting aside her mourning and anguish for a later time. A safer time. She needed to be fully and completely on the path to ending this crisis. Then she could face her demons.

She still came across a few mindless zombies being pulled along by the threads emerging from their heads. The few ghoulish arms and tentacles that sprouted from the walls and floors moved and held the obstacles aside, but most of their strength was gathered high above, and so to R'Bec's gratitude, they were unable to collect enough incidental mass to sever the threads and permanently slay them. Of course, it wouldn't matter if they could; these slaves had been dead for a long time. As awful as it was to watch them move—as jarring as it was to understand that they could not even feel the agony that would absolutely be justified if they could comprehend their current state—setting them free was the right thing to do. But her mind was torn as it was, she couldn't stand the thought of mercy-killing five, or ten, or however many of these things there were between her and their master. Not until she, too, was free.

R'Bec turned the corner. Although it was difficult to see very far, even with the red emergency lighting, there appeared to be a fork coming up ahead. For most of the way here, she had followed the trail of corpses, but even those were wearing thin. Which shouldn't make sense—there should be more of those monsters here than further away. This was where they were being pulled to. Regardless, she couldn't dwell on it too much. She only hoped something would be present to guide her the rest of the way; she had to imagine, and hope, that she was nearing her goal.

A step forward. Then her knees buckled, and she recoiled forward in shock. A sharp pain rang through her head, sending her whole body forward at the sudden inflammation. Her hands came up to clutch her temples. A stinging like this had only occurred once before: when Titan Black had crashed through her shield that she had bound inside her mind. That day proved that a powerful enough force could break her illusions, but even more concerning, that such an act could hurt her.

But she had no permanent illusions in place right now, other than her clothes, and her wall at home. The wall, though— that brick wall with the spray-painted planet which concealed her humble studio—was not broken, she knew that to be true. All of her senses, all of the synapses in her mind agreed that it was intact. No, the illusion that was dispelled was something far larger and more significant, something made permanent by its own will.

A very large nightmare was just destroyed on the surface. That dissolution reverberated back into the subconscious recesses of her mind, and because it was so large and controlled such a significant portion of her illusory powers, that imaginary pain became real, and struck at the only thing that it could.

But that also allowed R'Bec's nightmares to pick up on what was going on. They didn't need to be out in the desert anymore—they couldn't torment her there. And now with a vast majority of their allotted existence shattered, they could return to her side.

As a hand reached out from the pool of black sludge that had almost instantaneously formed on the corridor floor, eagerly grabbing her ankle, she broke into a run down the hallway.

The red light had been dim, yes, but it was still light. It still had worked to illuminate the area, if only nearest the bulbs. But even that was being drowned out. The shadows of her mind leaked out from the corners of the walls, splashing all over the floor and ceiling. The unease of the darkness was only supplemented further by the eerie glow of those purple nodes buried within.

She ran through the violet hall, trying with all of her might to banish the nightmares back again, back and away from her. But it was no use now. They were here to stay, and they would make sure she knew it.

More hands reached out for R'Bec's legs, trying to pull her to the ground. Faces lunged at her from the walls, screaming and biting at her as she passed. She turned at the fork—she didn't even know which direction, much less if it would be correct. She only wanted to flee, knowing deep down that there would never be an escape for her.

But she had to do something. She couldn't run forever, and she knew now that they could be tricked.

No.

She knew that they could be *controlled*.

She had willed them to conglomerate on the surface. She told them to go away from her. She shouldn't have been able to do that, she now realized, and yet it worked. Even if they weren't listening now, she had some say in their actions.

Because, of course, they weren't just nightmares. They were *her* nightmares.

She stopped.

The horrors took the opportunity to reach out for her as much as they wanted, totally unfettered. Faces and rats bit at her ankles and feet, gnashing through the illusions of her shoes. Tentacles stretched impossibly from the floor and crawled up her thighs, as fingers and arms poked out of the walls—which closed in on her with more of the congealed mass of agony—to pinch her stomach and tighten around her chest, ignoring the protective layer of her imagined clothes and even the real torn dress she still wore. Lapping tongues and snapping claws brought even her hair into the mix, tugging at it with fervor and pulling it out of the way to pester her scalp. It was torture.

But even still, through all of her imagined anxieties and fears and discomforts, she worked. R'Bec closed her eyes, held her head, and reached into her mind. She pulled together all of her rational thoughts, her senses; but more than that, she collected those unwanted portions, too. She brought together, perhaps for

204

the first time in her life, *truly* every synapse in her brain. Those irrational feelings and emotions, working in tandem with what she knew well enough already. She was determined to create the most perfect mental binding of all time, to permanently lock away her nightmares. Because this time, her nightmares would be included—more than that, they were going to help.

She couldn't see. She couldn't even hear. All of her mental capacity was drawn inside, now, intent on completing this internal architecture. She looked deep inside herself, pulling together the horrors that had haunted her for all her life. Mister Snuggles, Squeaky McFarts, even Fuzzywuzzymuffin all became compliant pieces of their own restraints. Without looking, or listening, or even feeling, she allowed her mind to harmonize and to recognize that the monsters and fears that surrounded her were being drawn back inside.

Banishing was not enough—she saw that now. The nightmares were more than just hers to control, they were her responsibility. Even as part of her subconscious, even as they killed and destroyed and tortured against her conscious will, she was accountable for her mind. Their actions were her own. And she would make it right. Because once she understood that, they did, too.

R'Bec opened her eyes.

The hallway was red again. The shadows had been pulled away from the walls. There was no purple glow from anywhere, faded through black ooze or otherwise.

But of course, the nightmares weren't gone. They never could be. It was foolish to think she could ever pretend they didn't exist—it only ever gave them more power over her, always living in fear that they might fester up again.

She touched her finger to her neck, just above her collar.

A new necklace had been summoned there, just as she imagined.

She couldn't bend her neck enough to see it, but R'Bec knew exactly what it looked like. The choker was of a wide, thin band that tightly hugged her illusory Native American skin. At the front, an opal-like shape served as the focal point for the piece of jewelry. But it was not jewelry. The whole thing was made up of the substance that her nightmares wore: that hazy black jelly with purple lights pulsating just beneath the surface, dancing with no apparent purpose. Her nightmares were contained there—not as a prison, but as a manifestation of her responsibility. R'Bec's mind was whole again.

And now, she would use that newfound control to end this misery and put to rest the wandering bodies of the long-dead.

The pattering of decaying skin on the floor ahead told R'Bec that, thankfully, she was still on the right track.

In fact, as she moved closer, she thought that she might finally be at the end of the line. The sound grew, and became accompanied by other noises that became more violent with every step. Metal scraping metal, breaking glass and glittering shards, and dry flesh slapping flesh.

The hallway ended at a large set of double doors. She quietly pushed through them, and entered the expansive new room.

The space appeared to be some great hangar. It had large doors at the other end, which she presumed could slide open for whatever aircraft was contained within. But that didn't make much sense; this was underground! Perhaps not terribly deep, but surely too far for a functional hangar.

The lights were on in here, the room seemingly exempt from the red glow of the emergency systems that flooded the rest of the facility. The white sterility did its best to illuminate the huge expanse of darkness, but there were still some patches that were difficult to peer into.

Fortunately, the chamber's focal point was plenty well-lit.

In the middle of the room lay a strange, alien craft, unlike anything R'Bec had ever seen. It was mostly of a wiry design, made up of thin metal poles that arced and twisted to create a cone shape. In a few places where circles intersected with crossbars, tiny rooms were locked in place, although they appeared to be able to slide along the surface of the frame. Engines at the back, and a very obvious bridge-like room that appeared only big enough for two people to sit down in told her that she was looking at a modular spaceship, and one that was clearly not built here.

But it wasn't alone in the hangar. An army of zombies, almost as numerous as the one that swarmed the Cosmopolitan only hours ago, surrounded the machine. They climbed over each other and clambered around and over the unique shape, ripping and tearing and scrounging for its precious metal. The material of the ship was hardy and resilient—it took some effort for even the fast and strong corpses to remove the smallest of chunks. They were harvesting it, collecting it, just as with the marconium battery.

And from the mess of enslaved horrors stretched an incalculable clutter of thin black threads, reaching out of the backs of their heads and arcing all around the room. They moved and shook with an almost amused twinge at every motion of their pained, ignorant puppets. Even still, it was no difficult task to follow them to their source. The strings led back to the fingers of an equally grey-skinned—but not decayed—man.

He was of a different state than his servants. Although he shared the same tone of flesh, he was not hunched or pained as they were. He faced away from R'Bec, and was some thirty feet into the room, but she could see clearly enough that his cargo pants were immaculate, and the vest he wore which showed his arms—and that R'Bec guessed was likely open in the front, judging on what she could make of the man's personality from this first impression—was unscathed. His arms looked to be tattooed with rips and tears, and his black hair stood on end, as though it were styled to be as menacing as possible—in a goofy, boyish sort of way.

She stepped into the expanse. Slowly, so as not to provoke the zombie master, but not in such a way that he wouldn't know she was there. Her intentional lack of stealth, therefore, did not go unnoticed.

"You're a persistent little girl, aren't you?" he said. His voice was shrill and cold, but his tone was one of condescension. At his pauses, R'Bec recognized a hint of his pained breath. Controlling so many bodies must take a lot out of him. "You're the one who tried to stop me at the Cosmopolitan, right? Pretty fancy footwork, my dear."

"My *name* is Lady— err, R'Bec. You can call me R'Bec, villain."

He shrugged. "I don't think I'll call you anything. Get out of here, I don't have time for you. We're on a very tight schedule."

"What do I call you?" She had to try to keep him talking. The more she understood, the better she'd be able to formulate how to handle this. She could feel her doubt and uncertainty blurring the edges of her nightmares' cage; she had to maintain composure and control.

"I don't think you heard me. Leave." The man turned his head to glance back at her—his eyes were the same black pools of his slaves, and just as impossibly unreflective. As he did so, he flinched one of his fingers, tugging at some of the strings extending out from it. A few of the zombies looked at her too, though didn't make a move beyond that.

Recognizing that R'Bec wasn't leaving, he sighed and gave in. "The name's Jet Wicked. Necromancer."

"I've seen how these things work. You're not reviving them, you're just pulling them along. Are you an alien?"

Jet laughed. "You're funny. No, just because I'm in Area 51 doesn't make me an alien. I'm human, just... a better human, with a very special skill. I saw that you have a very special skill, too. Was it you behind those disgusting creatures? Well don't even think about it. I have experience with the unseemly, so again, I invite you to leave me alone and let me perform my work."

"What is your work?" R'Bec asked without missing a beat. He wasn't attacking her, which she hoped meant that he couldn't. If nothing else, he seemed to have enough honor—or naiveté—to answer her questions, if shown enough persistence.

"I'm a collector; I'm retrieving powerful machinery for a very important project." Wicked said, sighing again. "This Telignen ship has some of the most advanced computing technology and strongest metal alloys on Earth right now, so I'm... relieving these soldiers of its burden."

Did she hear right? This was a Telignen ship? Legacy was a liar and a monster, but there was no reason for her to mislead

209

R'Bec in telling her that no Telignen had left Peplorix, much less come to Earth, other than her family. So how did this get here?

"Well, Jet, you might be human, but I'm not. I'm a Telignen." With this new information, and confidence gained from this declaration, she had the beginnings of a plan of attack in place.

With careful timing and placement, R'Bec began to summon new illusions in the room: creatures that looked identical to Jet Wicked's own horde. One by one, new zombies joined his swarm, complete with imaginary threads leading back to his fingers.

"Oh, really?" he replied, again turning his head in interest. His attention diverted, R'Bec summoned even more make-believe corpses to 'serve' the necromancer. They climbed on their real counterparts and swiped at pieces of the spaceship with equal abandon, not giving away their loyalties yet. "I admit, I don't know much about it. That's just what my master told me when he sent me here."

"Your master?" she asked with false curiosity. Although it was an interesting surprise, she didn't really care to whom or where his allegiance was pledged. R'Bec only needed more material to keep him talking, as she continued to add more traitors to his army.

"You don't think power like this comes naturally, do you? Sure, it took a lot of practice, but it was all thanks to my master's blessings."

Wicked's head remained at an angle, his impossibly black eyes held on R'Bec behind him. He couldn't tell that his throng had nearly doubled in size, nor that almost half of the horde *behaved* like the others, but did not twitch and writhe with the motions of his itchy fingers.

This was her opportunity. With a casual thought, she bid her illusions to break the charade and attack the undead puppeteer.

All at once, nearly fifty zombies leapt from the crowd, turning from the actual corpses and the ship. They jumped and climbed over the rest of the assemblage of decaying limbs, making their way for Jet Wicked.

His head turned in shock at the new noises. He clenched his fingers back into fists, pulling on all of his strings in silent instruction. "Defend me!" he shouted in additional order.

The army of the undead took their hands and mouths off of the metal craft, too, and their attention shifted just as their master's did to the apparent traitors.

"This is your doing! Isn't it?" Jet screamed over the gargled roars of the monsters and reflections. Nearly evenly matched, his black-eyed slaves fought tooth and nail against R'Bec's own illusory horde. He was clearly straining himself, having to adjust from comfortable supervision to commanding a battle. He waved his arms all around him, trying to turn his body for a greater range of motion and visibility. His fingers moved independently of one another, almost unnaturally so, as he tugged at the threads of his corpses.

His motions didn't seem to be for show, but as R'Bec approached slowly from behind, she noted that his pawns did have some agency. None were fighting perfectly in unison. That only made the horror of their enslavement that much more tragic.

But she kept on anyway, determined to move against the necromancer. His attention was largely diverted; he was aware of her presence, but wasn't expecting a direct assault. The Telignen came up behind him and harshly brought her fist up and into his side, just beneath his lowest rib.

He howled in pain, the loss of wind and balance sending him down to the floor. As he fell, his fingers stretched out in an instinctive attempt to catch himself, releasing some of his control on the zombies, though he still held onto their threads. Without such aggressive instruction, R'Bec's false swarm gained an advantage in the skirmish. Her reflections held the corpses down on the floor, and she willed them to swipe and snap at the threads extending from them with extreme prejudice.

A few of Wicked's strings were broken with great effort—to R'Bec's eyes, only with the combined strength of two or three of her illusions—but before too long the man's adrenaline seemingly kicked in. He tugged on the strings once more, even despite his attacker's heel pressing into his bare chest, revealed by his open black vest. With the new orders, a small group of his servants quickly descended upon the woman, pulling her off of him. Similarly, another pair of the indentured corpses helped him to his feet.

Although Jet's eyes were without depth or sheen, their weight grew in terror as his grey face twisted around them, becoming one of rage. In a fit, he once again clenched his fists and dragged his arms down to his sides, pulling harshly on the strings extending from his fingers.

This act seemed to do more than just increase his control of the horde. They became visibly and demonstrably stronger. The threads which spread out inside their bodies and writhed beneath their skin expanded somewhat, giving them the power necessary to dissolve their imaginary doppelgangers.

R'Bec kicked away the zombies holding her hostage, who preferred to join their fellow slaves in the battle than attempt to recapture her. Jet Wicked was now surrounded by a small personal guard of ghouls, anyway.

She returned to her thoughts, summoning more of her illusions to fight the swarm of undead. She tried to match their strength, conjuring larger and more muscular reflections to face the real things. But despite their size, their strength was still well outclassing what she could imagine. Her illusions were holding their own better, but not by much.

Unable to count on the brutish fantasies to be able to sever the binds from Wicked to zombie, R'Bec knew she had to join in the fight, too.

She thought back to the Cosmopolitan. She had used twin swords there, not guns. When she swung them wildly in an attempt to inflict as much damage as she could to the bodies of the corpses, she was able to fell a few. Remembering and reimagining those moments, she understood how: she wasn't hurting them enough to kill them, she was accidentally waving her blades in the line of the then-unnoticed threads, cutting them.

With this newfound knowledge, she once again conjured two razor-thin swords in her hands, and entered the forays of the undead clash with her imagination.

She was able to attack with more freedom and awareness, but she bound what illusions she could into permanence with her mind in an attempt to give them better resistance from reality. Hopefully the more persistent fake zombies would require more focus from Wicked to defeat, which might in turn give her safer passage as she attempted to slice at his connections.

She jumped and turned in mid-air, spinning her swords with abandon. A few times, her blade briefly caught on a near-invisible force, which easily broke to her superior strength.

Several of the necromancer's horde fell limp after only a few seconds of her tirade. But with even further tightening of his fingers—which already grew darker in apparent pain and internal self-mutilation—the threads learned to fight back.

When R'Bec once again hopped up to give her access to the strings protruding from a group of zombies' necks, her sword caught as last time. But the connection did not yield.

Her momentum and balance lost, she fell on her back in the middle of a crowd of undead. They looked down at her with hunger, the cold voids of their eyes more menacing than ever. Their arms stretched down, eager to pull her apart.

She summoned a small ring above her, which grew and expanded out, pushing the small gathering away from her before it dissolved. A handle imagined above her helped R'Bec quickly pull herself back to her feet, and she began to conjure floating steps to jump above and over the chaotic skirmish.

Jet Wicked was some distance away, now. Evidently, proximity to his slaves did nothing to affect his control of them; those horrors furthest away from him fought just as efficiently as those that sought to protect him.

On top of that, R'Bec's false zombies did not appear to achieve her desired goal. The necromancer's self-awareness clearly extended to his minions, and so there were no instances of his own undead attacking one-another. However, his eyes—and those of his slaves, which R'Bec presumed he could see through to some degree—could still play tricks on him. Several times, his horde did not become immediately aware of her new illusions peppering the battlefield, and so they could move towards his center of control unhindered. She therefore made an effort to summon new, mentally-bound zombies closer to him, hoping that if enough could reach his closest guards that she might end the fight in one fell swoop.

As she did so, R'Bec imagined two much greater swords in her hands. Hoping the increase in size and power would be enough to break through Wicked's ties to the zombies, she began flailing those around just as before, leaping from one newly summoned platform to the next over the sea of undead.

The necromancer would not allow even an attempt at this course of action without a fight. He raised his arms up, giving him even more of the appearance of a puppeteer controlling his marionettes. However, instead of lifting the zombies into the air to dance at his behest, the strings that stretched from Jet's fingers rose up, out of reach of R'Bec's swords even as she hopped upon her pedestals.

She fought harder and brought herself higher as she strained to see if her new blades were capable of cutting the threads, but Jet Wicked was more focused on protecting his handiwork now, clearly aiming to wear the Telignen out.

As both battles raged on—as R'Bec silently ordered her illusions to clamber over the animated corpses in a desperate attempt to sever their ties to the necromancer; as the very real zombies took advantage of the illusions' diverted focus to more aggressively attack and dissolve them; as she ran and jumped far and high for the slightest graze of Wicked's puppet strings—she grew more and more exhausted. She was struggling to gather the effort to continue her tantrum through the air. Her body didn't produce adrenaline in the same way as humans, or perhaps if it did, the effects were wearing off. Fear and stress began to take hold, and she could feel the edges of her new necklace fading once again, the nightmares extending into tiny teeth, pressing against her.

Seizing the opportunity for a counteroffensive, Jet flicked his thumb and commanded one of his threads to part from the mass of twisted strings swirling about the room. It stretched and extended outward, then back around and down to R'Bec's level. She didn't have time to register it; jumping between one hovering platform and the next, the necromantic string caught on her extended foot, tripping her balance. Her intended landing zone dissipated at the lack of attention, as did her swords, and she plummeted back to the ground and into the mass of decaying punches and kicks.

Again, in the corners of her vision, R'Bec could see the approach of her opponent's minions, eager to taste her alien flesh. As tears welled in her eyes, she found herself out of options.

Release.

With a solemn blink of her eyes, she let go of those ties that bound her power inside the imaginary jewelry around her neck. Her nightmares became freed once more.

But this time, it would be Jet Wicked that felt their torment, not her. They were her tools now—they were *her*. All of her fears and inadequacies given form by her gift as a Telignen, and they served her mind. She understood now—she was responsible for them, and now they recognized this too.

Instantly, the walls and floor became slathered with the grotesque slime and purple lights. Arms reached out of the ooze excitedly; much larger arms than before, at R'Bec's silent request. They lifted and crushed Wicked's zombies in their grasp. Spiders and rats and pelicans dotted the landscape of the hangar, tearing apart the necromancer's zombies. It was easy for them—all those years building up in the dark corners of her mind, R'Bec's nightmares were more powerful than anything she could possibly imagine on a whim. The perfect final resort.

As Jet's army wore thin, unable to defend against the full, unhindered force of the Telignen's mind in harmony, he found himself cowering behind what few zombies were left nearby. He tugged at the strings of the few dozen other ghouls still lingering in the mess, as if to beg them to protect him.

But they would do no such thing.

With a guttural, primal scream of emotion—fueled by her rage for Legacy's betrayal, for Kicks' injury, and most pertinent, for Jenna's murder—she willed her nightmares to expand in an explosion of imagined tentacles and limbs. Spikes and fingers and frills reached out from every corner of the room, aiming for every single one of the necromancer's threads thrice over. In a single moment, all of Wicked's connections were cut; the corpses that they held up fell limp, finally freed of their service to the tyrant.

Quickly, R'Bec recollected her thoughts, gathering all of her synapses and binding her nightmares together into her opal-adorned choker once again. Then, for good measure, she summoned two metal gloves—bound and made permanent inside her mind—to encase Jet Wicked's hands. He tried to release more strings from his fingers, but her mental blocks were resolute against his power without the strength of a host.

He knelt on the floor, sulking and defeated.

R'Bec approached, and summoned in her hand her most favorite illusion: her iconic oversized pistol.

One target.

One very real bullet.

She held the chamber to Jet's head, point blank. He looked up with his impossibly black eyes, as if to beg her for mercy. But he couldn't speak. She knew that *he* knew, if he tried, that she would fire before he even finished his first syllable.

R'Bec clenched her trigger finger.

She was ready. It was time.

"Alright, asshole. This is for Jenna."

There was no click. There was no pop or explosion, nor a ringing to her ears. She had closed her eyes in an expectant flinch, but there was no brightness burnt through her eyelids.

Instead, she found herself pushed backward some distance. Her illusory shoes scraped against the cool concrete floor, slowing her to a stop, before she fell onto her back.

R'Bec looked up, struggling to get to her feet at first. Between her and Jet Wicked, where they had just been standing, hovered a shining purple man.

At first glance, that is. It looked like a man, and it looked purple. As her eyes refocused, R'Bec was able to get a better look at the figure. It floated there idly, as if the act of flight required no physical strain or mental focus. It had the silhouette of a man without clothes—though lacking any signs of gender outside of general build. R'Bec wasn't convinced it was a man, though. Largely, because it was not opaque.

The being appeared to be comprised of a violet or magenta translucent light, with small specks of white light dancing unsupported within its frame. It had no other physical traits; no hair, clothes, or even surface features, with the exception of its face.

Although it faced away from her, towards the necromancer, R'Bec could make out that its eyes, mouth, and nose were also made up of the white light which was contained within it, rather than the same purple hue of the rest of its body. There were no pupils or lips. Only the light.

"Jet Wicked." the radiant being spoke. Its voice was sharp and impressive. She couldn't place the accent—although it spoke English, the inflections and pronunciations were not quite like any other on Earth. One thing that R'Bec was certain of, however, was that it sounded perfect. Superior. Almost... divine.

"What's it to ya, buddy?" the necromancer challenged, waving a metal-encased fist at the hovering figure.

"I am Corpsegaze. I am the incarnation and protector of the laws of death. You have been found guilty of willful and malicious disregard for these laws in your practice of necromancy on such an extensive scale. The stability of reality is threatened by your actions, and so your punishment shall be an immediate demise."

The dispassionate alien raised an arm against the human, its hand starting to glow as an apparent attack quickly charged.

Before it released whatever burst of energy it was planning, Wicked ceased his cowering and replaced it with a sickening cackle.

"You— oh god, you stupid aliens. You morons, you can't put anything together, can you?" he laughed, slapping the ground with glee. His metal restraints clanged against the floor, which echoed across the hangar. "You can't freakin' *kill* me! Just as I can raise the dead, so too can my master. And so he has done, *to me*. I am immortal, undying, imperishable! And there's nothing you can do to stop me!"

Corpsegaze lowered its arm, accepting Wicked's words as fact. "Then you will be erased from existence, and your master will be discovered and given the same fate. The stability of reality and its laws cannot be hindered by you or anyone." Its whole body began to glow now, as it apparently gathered all of the force afforded it as a cosmic being, preparing to completely annihilate the necromancer.

However, again, its divinity was too slow. R'Bec saw a cloud of swirling smoke and shadows descend from the poorly-lit ceiling. It dripped and fluttered down like some strange collection of Jet's own puppet strings, although clearly distinct, and more organic in their unified, fluid motions.

The cloud surrounded and encased Jet Wicked, whose manic laughter could still be heard through the shadowy smoke. It lifted him—and a few scattered pieces of the Telignen spacecraft—before bounding out of the double doors from where R'Bec had entered, like some wild animal leaping through the wilderness in escape.

Jet Wicked was gone. And, presumably, so was the marconium core.

R'Bec expected Corpsegaze to pursue him and the mysterious shadow creature, but instead, it turned to face *her*, now.

"Lady Harrow."

"It's R'Bec. And don't you try to pull anything on me, I haven't broken any laws of reality."

"Apologies." It bowed its head in momentary shame as it floated closer to her, descending enough to still hover above her, but stand on somewhat more even footing to the mortal Telignen. "And indeed. You sought to protect reality, by eliminating the threat of the necromancer, whether you understood that as your mission or not."

"You're welcome." she replied, unsure of where this was going. She wasn't interested in a medal, she wanted to go after Wicked and make him pay.

"Thank you, yes." Corpsegaze paused, though whether it was involuntary or in hesitation was unclear to her. "I came at this time in the hopes of handling the issue of Jet Wicked. But he was not the only reason I came. I had hoped you would show me what I knew to lie inside of you, and you did."

R'Bec cocked her head and furrowed her brow in confusion. "I don't understand."

It extended its arm out again, only this time, it was with open palm up, in invitation. "You have shown courage and responsibility, as well as power, that we seek in a time of need. I invite you... No, I humbly request that you accompany me, to meet with my brothers and I. We have a proposition to make of you. A chance to have your vengeance against Jet Wicked, yes; but more importantly, a chance to serve a greater cause."

Things were moving quickly for R'Bec. The room was spinning inside her head. She felt dizzy. She felt empowered. She felt betrayed.

Corpsegaze had interrupted her. Its actions cost her the victory—the closure—that she had earned. She'd only just beaten her own mind, and now she was being asked to go who-knows-where to hear out a cosmic being. It was nonsense.

But, everything that she'd gone through tonight weighed heavily on her mind. R'Bec had lost a lot in only the past few hours, but she'd achieved a lot, too. She'd lost an unexplored love interest, but she also escaped a toxic relationship built on lies, and found some peace with her past and her own sanity. Despite this failure, this temporary setback, she was in a good place.

Corpsegaze's hand was still held out for her. She looked up at its shining face of faultless violet light. It was a face of beauty and perfection, fitting for a being of such stature. It was welcoming and reassuring.

She touched the nightmarish necklace bound to her skin and to her mind, reassuring herself for the last time that she was in control.

"Alright, I'll agree to at least hear you out. But no promises."

She set her hand down in Corpsegaze's. Evidently, this notion was enough for it. It closed its fingers firmly around her significantly smaller hand and wrist, carefully but securely holding her still. It began to hover up, carrying the Telignen with it.

As they reached the ceiling, R'Bec and Corpsegaze phased through the several feet of concrete, and then further through the immeasurable amount of stone, dirt, and sand. They passed through it all without any disturbance, as though reality itself bent in deference to the entity.

Once they escaped the claustrophobic earth, they continued to fly higher in the early morning sky of the Nevada desert. R'Bec glanced down at the space below them—at Area 51 and Groom Lake, still eerily lit by small fires from her earlier immolation. Although as they rose higher still, it became harder and harder to see the specks of light dotting the base.

She could just barely see the very edges of the sun reaching over the horizon, which grew more round and faded with every second that the two creatures that were not of this world rose into the heavens, and into space, towards wherever Corpsegaze intended on taking the one it knew as Lady Harrow.

Epilogue

Wallace and Levin stood on either side of the pair of double doors, backs against the concrete wall and empty weapons readied. Kicks held his breath beside the younger officer, while the airmen stayed back some distance.

The nightmares had vanished once they gathered themselves in the dim catacombs of Area 51. Kicks joined shortly thereafter, eager to share his triumph against the apparent root of the evil. Continuing down the hallways, still lit only by the red glow of the emergency, it became clear that whatever they were going to find at the end, the threat was gone and resolved.

Dead zombies marked their path and lead them further into the militant abyss. Their decayed forms were not so horrifying up close. It was almost sad.

Their eyes sat empty in their skulls, the skin pulled tightly as if in twisted pain. Their bony, outstretched arms were flailed at their sides, creating a minefield of rot and flesh for the hunting party to tiptoe through.

And finally, they came upon the door. The airmen attempted to order Detective Wallace to ignore it and turn back, but their authority fell on deaf ears. He demanded answers, and the trail leading here promised just that. And perhaps, they had the same morbid curiosity.

With a silent nod to his trusted partner, they turned the handles and quickly opened the doors in tandem, training their weapons at the expanse. Although they had run out of bullets some time ago, the threat of harm was sometimes still enough to deescalate a situation.

It was a vast hangar, much more brightly lit than the corridors they had just emerged from. Large hangar doors dominated the far side of the room, despite their apparent location underground. In the middle of the room lay a strange, wiry structure. A metal machine with curved rods and room-like spheres all around it. The vehicle—it seemed a vehicle, judging by the cone shape and what appeared to be a driver's seat in the front sphere, like a cockpit—was dilapidated and torn apart. Pieces were scattered about, and those still attached were bent and snapped at the joints.

Dozens of bodies were also scattered about the concrete floor of the hangar. The same grey corpses that had brought them here, whose defeated forms lead them through the darkness and into this room, sprawled out in terrible, frozen agony. Whatever had animated them was long-gone.

Wallace turned his head to read the faces of his allies. Levin seemed concerned and frustrated, though his breathing indicated relief above all. Kicks was clearly struggling not to again shout "I told you so."

"What the hell happened here?" Colton finally said to no one in particular.

"Something unique, Detective." a new voice shouted from behind them, echoing unfamiliarly in the large chamber. Wallace— and his two associates—turned in place to face the double doors again.

The woman entering the room was composed. Her black pantsuit and shining high heels were distractingly out of place in the underground base. Her long black hair was tied in a ponytail, framing and displaying her Asian complexion. She was old, but her confidence and authority masked her age.

"Something very unique, and something way out of your league." she finished, stepping fully into the light shining on the unusual heap of metal. She extended a hand, and Colton reached out to shake it with unease. "Daisy Shim."

"Detective Colton Wallace." he replied to the woman who he presumed already knew his name, somehow. "What do you mean by that? Who are you?"

"I work for the United Nations, Detective." Shim said, returning her hand to her back, folded with the other behind her. "What happened here is a matter of world security, and cannot leave this room."

"Oh shit, she's gonna kill us!" Kicks worried aloud.

"Relax, Mister Cortez. No one else is dying today."

Kicks took a step back and slumped down slightly at the use of his surname.

"So what are you doing here, ma'am? What do you want with this—with us?" Levin asked.

"With this abandoned spaceship? I want to contain it, and make sure these monsters never see the light of day, or the front of a newspaper." Shim stepped over to one of the nearby corpses, peering down at it without the courtesy to crouch at all. "With you? I want to offer you a job. All of you."

"Doing what?" Wallace asked on his friends' behalf.

"Exactly what you were doing here: investigating unique situations. Only, working for me, you'll actually be successful."

Wallace took a few extra moments to process Ms. Shim's words. He looked around again in awe and apology at the collection of limp horrors around him, and then at the mysterious machine they were apparently trying to tear apart.

Lady Harrow wasn't here. The marconium was nowhere to be found. The nightmarish creatures had vanished without a trace. And it was unclear whether these corpses had completed whatever dark mission they came here for. He had no answers at all. Only failures and theories, slipping through his hands and out of sight.

His gaze returned to Daisy Shim. With a silent nod, he stretched his own hand out for her. In the corner of his eye, he saw both Victor and Kicks shuffle in place some, but in turn they both nodded in agreement with Colton's action.

Ms. Shim accepted his handshake, confirming her proposal. The entourage proceeded silently out of the hangar, bound for a destination far away from the base at Groom Lake.

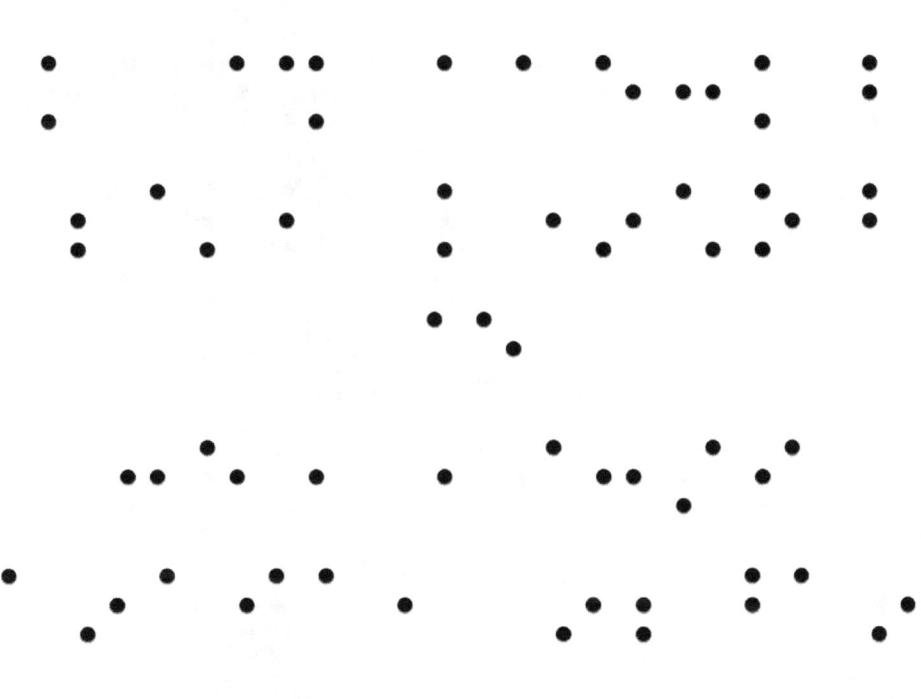

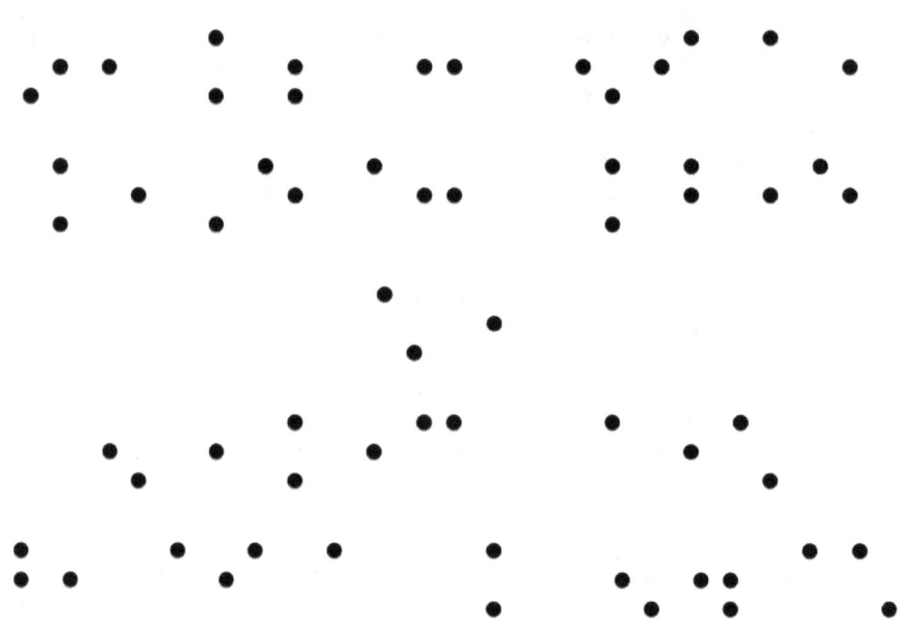

About the Author

Robert grew up in Phoenix, Arizona, where he began imagining unique stories of superheroes and villains in fantastic tales told orally to his friends and family.

For nearly eight years, these characters remained only in his head before he took to  writing down the first adventures of the universe he had crafted, taking extra care in the realism of both the science-fiction aspects as well as in the emotion and psychology of people at their most powerful—and most vulnerable.

Starting with *Shatterbug*, he hopes to tell a wide-reaching story to unite and inspire people, not under one common ideal of what the world should be like, but against the shared understanding of what the world should not be.

Robert currently lives in Cincinnati, Ohio, but hopes one day to return home to the desert.

Find Robert on Facebook and Twitter: @RobDukeOfficial

www.ingramcontent.com/pod-product-compliance
Lightning Source LLC
Chambersburg PA
CBHW021029130626
46552CB00005B/1757